Ungodly Soul Ties II
"The Struggle"

Andrea E. Lawrence

Dedication

I dedicate this book to my revelation of pain, because it birthed passion. In order for passion to be revealed pain had to be experienced. I am in a great place, because I learned how to emerge from my hurt, heartaches and disappointments. I learned to have unshakeable faith and genuine forgiveness, so I wouldn't become like the ones who hurt me. They said I would never... But God said OH! Did she ever, who's smiling now? Me.

One Love!

Acknowledgments

Thank you, my Heavenly Father. Holy is your name. If it wasn't for you, I would not be who I am. Without you, I am nothing.

Thanks, Mom, Dad and sis for your love.

Thank you Sha-kil and Samiyah Lawrence, my lovely children. I love you both so much for your love, prayers, honesty, emotional support, and patience during our struggle. My Blessed Fruit.

I want to give a special shot out to my spiritual sisters and home - girls Dr. T'Onya Green, Natalie Hinds – Scott , Dr. Kandice Cooper, Leah Wells, Shakirah Morgan and Audry Terrell Hughes for being there for me whenever I needed y'all. I appreciate you all love, prayers, support and listening ear no matter what time I called you ladies. I cannot forget my daughter from another mother Ashley Jaynese Taylor, no limits baby girl. God Bless!

Thank you to my family members and everyone who supported me, your act of kindness has not been overlooked. I appreciate you all greatly.

Last but not least, to the author and finisher of my faith, Jesus, I thank you for relationship and religion. Love you!

Introduction

Twinkle continues to struggle with deep-rooted issues within herself. She has played with fire, got burnt, broken and purified. However the devil is not backing down and is still seeking to destroy her life with a vengeance.

Although Sly is appearing to be a changed man the evidence of his shed skin is a constant reminder that a snake is still a snake. Nevertheless her faith in God believes that anyone can change.

Readers can expect to enjoy Twinkle's spiritual journey of struggle as it continues.

Table of Contents

Chapter 1
The Struggle

Am I schizin', buggin', wildin' or what?

This ghost called fantasy won't let me be. Yeah! I know I repeated the prayers, but real talk I still want and miss this dude.

Y'all already know who it is, and for those who don't know, it's that boy Sly. Dang! What's going on with me?

Were his looks and shot really that good to me? Or am I just feenin', because I'm trying to remain free? I really do know better, but breaking this curse called "lust" is straight crazy to me. Can it really be done? So far yes! Because I still ain't got none, but real talk, I want some.

This thing is easier said than done. What do you do when your heart no longer loves him, but your flesh still does? Sheesh! Even the condom commercials got me feeling some type of way. Oh yeah! I'm back.

It's me, Twinkle.

In the hospital laying in Room 712 B in the middle of May, I can hardly breathe, do to double pneumonia. The woman in the bed beside me has Alzheimer's and she's been moaning and talking to herself all night. Her eyes are old and rheumy. She is shriveled in the bed in a fetal position and her corpselike energy feels like she's touched with a little poltergeist. I think these meds have me hallucinating. Nah! I take that back. No they don't. I just want to get the hell out of here.

I was admitted to the hospital three days ago and was diagnosed with Community Acquired Pneumonia. What the heck is that? All I know is that I have major problems with breathing, talking and I'm running a very high fever that won't break. My head feels like its spinning and my lungs feels like an elephant just kicked me in my chest.

Originally I thought I had H1N1 (Swine Flu), because I was feeling so bad. You all remember that one year when people were dying from the swine flu it was major.

Right now, I feel lifeless and alone wondering why God knocked me on my behind. My spirit keeps telling me that God wants me to listen to him without distraction.

My parents are watching Anisa, she is now ten years old and Shaquan is seventeen years old. I asked my parents not to mention this to anyone and could they just pray for me. I didn't want anyone to know, because I didn't want to be overwhelmed with phone calls and visits from family members that are only being nosey. You know the family members who truly care for you and you know the ones who don't.

Of course, my parents didn't honor my request. As quick as I told them not to; my Dad told everyone. Then he had the guts to tell family members, "Twinkle told me not

11

to tell you, but I'm going to tell you anyway. She is in the hospital with double pneumonia." How do I know this? I learned my Dad told my cousin in front of my children and Shaquan told me. Wow! Really Dad!

As sick as I was I had to call and ask my Dad why he didn't honor my request. His response was out of respect for my cousin she needed to know, because she had come over to bring my mother flowers. Oh! By the way! My Mom was in the hospital for two days because she had a mini stroke.

God is good. My mother is not paralyzed, nor does she have any memory loss. When she was released I was admitted into the hospital.

Okay back to what I was saying. What does someone giving my mom flowers have to do with me and my request? Where is the loyalty and respect for your daughter? Ha! I guess there is none and when I asked my dad this question. He responded, "He is not going to allow people to dictate to him what he can do in his house." Wow! This was not about dictating. This is about love and respecting your number one daughter. Gasping for air, I whispered, "I'm sick Dad. I can hardly breathe, but you still find a way to upset me even on my sick bed."

When the phone call ended. Instantly, I started praying, "Heavenly Father, I need you. What is going on? Why are you showing me the heart of my family members right now? What I'm experiencing is hurtful and too much for me to handle right now. I am too weak for this. Why is it all of this confusion and strife? Why Lord! Answer me."

God answers back in a still voice, "Pray for those who hurt you and for those who despitefully use you."

"God I don't want to hear this."

Then my Heavenly Father reminded me in a whisper, "My child guard your heart, because that is where your treasure lies."

I started crying and asked God, "Why do I have to guard my heart against loved ones, especially my parents."

The Lord answered back, "Satan uses them the most, because they are the tune to your heart strings, emotions and feelings. My child, you can even have an *ungodly soul tie* to your parents. You must always love and honor them, but you cannot allow them to control your emotions. Break free my child from hurt, confusion, anger and pain. Break free my child and live the life I called you to live in, which is peace."

As tears flowed down my face, while lying on the hospital bed I said, "Father I will. Take this heart of mine and heal it from all my childhood hurts and pains."

Right then, the nurse walked in, "Lisa it's time for your nebulizer treatment." I quickly wiped my tears and sat up to start my treatment. This nurse was not very personable and her name had the nerve to be Kathy. When I would say "good morning" she would act like the word "good morning" was a foreign language. I think she had an attitude with me.

The day before, I told another nurse, Sherri, about my roommate disruption and peculiar noises. She was kind enough to take my roommate out of the room and had her sleep in the hallway for the entire night. Boy! I slept so well.

One of the nurse's aides got wind of it the next morning and she and another nurse's aid brought her back into the room. While they were putting her back into the bed this African American chick was talking so much ish. Mind you I can hear everything she is saying to the other aide. I guess they thought I was sleep, because my curtain was closed.

The African American chick continued, "Who does she think she is by having this lady sleep in the hallway all night?" Then whispered, "This B-ain't Beyoncé; she doesn't get no special treatment. Then followed up with, "I can't stand females like that, I'm going to talk to someone about this."

Did this African American nurse's aide just call me a B!@*$#? Yes she did. Right then I forcefully pulled my curtain open and yelled, "Tell whoever you want to tell chick. Who in the hell are you? I didn't request for my roommate to sit in the hallway all night. Your unprofessional wanna-be registered nurse. You and your friend get the hell out of my room. Now tell that!"

Right then her Caucasian co-worker intervenes, "Ma'am" in her valley girl voice. "She wasn't like talking about you. Like just calm down."

Angrily, I responded while mocking her. "Well, who was she talking about? In matter of fact, don't *like* even answer. *Like*, let your girl that had all of the mouth a minute ago, *like* answer."

They both stood there looking dumbfounded with nothing to say. I waited a few seconds and said, "You better recognize who I am. I'm not Beyoncé but I'm the girl Twinkle and if you don't know, now you know… dumb broads."

I don't know where my strength came from or how I was able to speak with that much energy. All I know is in that moment I was mad, and briefly forgot why I was in the hospital. They both looked at each other and walked out of the room.

My chest was painstaking; I still had trouble breathing and still was running a fever. However, I'm not going to allow anyone to punk me. Immediately, I called my ride or die and live sista Diamond, she was so ready. Nothing has changed, she is always ready to whoop someone's behind. Especially when it comes to me, she was at the hospital in 1.5 seconds.

When she arrived she said in her gangsta tone, "Sis! Show me who she is!"

At this time I started having problems breathing. I started gasping for air telling my sis in a hushed tone, "I'm good just chill."

Diamond responded, "Nah sis! These chicks need to know you have family support."

I wanted to laugh so badly, but my chest was hurting. I began to cry a little, "Diamond, my chest is on fire and I can hardly breathe." Diamond looked at me; I started to see her eyes beginning to get misty. She asked, "What's going on?"

"My body keeps rejecting the medicine and I'm constantly vomiting, as a result I'm not getting better." Every time I spoke I felt like I was taking my last breath. Diamond realized how weak I was and wanted to help me.

Seriously, "Diamond if God is ready to take me home then let it be."

Diamond, with authority, rose out of the chair and humbly said, "Jesus, I got turned up last night, so before I come into your presence I am begging for your forgiveness for all of my sins. Please don't allow what I'm about to ask you effect your decision, because of my sins.

However, my sister is sick; you said in your word that we are healed by your stripes. Heavenly Father you said ask me anything in your name Jesus and you will answer. Now I'm calling on you, because my sister is weak and she needs your healing power to overtake her body. I speak to my sister's spirit and I command her to live and not die and declare the works of the Lord. I cancel every assignment of the devil. I bind and cast him out in the name of Jesus. Jesus I ask you to give the Doctor's and Nurse's your wisdom to give my sister the medicine that her body will receive and not reject.

I ask you to dispatch your warring angels to protect her from anything and anyone that is not like you God. I pray that evil will not come nigh to her. My sister is one of your faithful servants. God give her the strength not to fight the battle, but to believe that you are God strong and mighty.

Remind her that you are Jehovah Rafa, which means you are a healer. Remind her that you are her present help when she is in trouble. Remind her that you love her and whatever she needs to learn from you while she is here; let her learn and then consistently apply it to her life in Jesus Name, In Jesus Name and together we said Amen."

After Diamond prayed immediately I went to sleep and didn't wake up until the next morning. While I was sleeping, I saw a man in my dreams. He looked celestial he gently brushed the left side of my face and said to me, "Get well." I remember him smiling at me and I smiled back at him. Right then, I knew that everything was going to be alright for me.

The next day a new doctor came in my room she was a beautiful Indian woman; we had a heart to heart talk. She stated, "That she is changing all of my meds," she continued to tell me, "My white blood cells were still high and this is the reason why my fever is not breaking."

I've been in this hospital for four days. Within these days my roommate has been constantly moaning. I'm getting tired of being hooked up to the IV, and the machine is constantly beeping. However, I was assured that God had finally sent me help.

My two joys just walked in, Shaquan and Anisa. Shaquan has grown so nicely he is 5'8, 165 pounds and buff. He thinks he is a jock, because he is a District Champ in wrestling and the girls think he is so handsome. I'm so excited that this is Shaquan's senior year.

Anisa is very beautiful and wise beyond her years. She praise dances, for those who don't know what that is, the correct name is liturgical dancing, which consist of dancing to gospel or positive music.

I love my children dearly and they both have smiles that can light up any room.

Shaquan in his deep voice asked, "Mom when are you coming home?"

"Hopefully tomorrow son."

Anisa chimed in, "good Mommy, because I miss you so much."

They stayed at the hospital for about an hour. Shaquan received his license and he thinks he is a fly guy. Wow! I can't believe my son is driving, how time flies. Shaquan enrolled into the Army so when he graduates from high school he will be going straight to boot camp. I always tried to keep my atmosphere and children's atmosphere free from drama. Negative energy is a waste and nothing good comes from it. I always taught my children great things happen when you distant yourself from negative people.

An hour had gone by, Shaquan said, "Mom we are about to leave." Anisa kissed my cheek and told me that she loved me. Before Shaquan left he kissed me and sincerely stated, "Mom I pray you come home tomorrow."

"I responded me too and I'll call y'all later."

When they left I started to feel lonely. I wanted to call Sly and tell him that I was in the hospital. However, the last time we talked it was on some other stuff because I was still angry from catching him and Pricy doing there one – two. After going back and forth in my mind about calling him I finally broke down and called.

Sly's phone rung several times, just before I hung up. Sly answers, "What's up?"

"Hey!" I answered back.

"Twinkle," he called my name in a startled pitch."

"Yeah it's me."

"What you have a new number," Sly asked?

"No, I'm in the hospital."

"Why!"

"I have double pneumonia."

"How did you get that Twinkle?"

"I don't know," I responded in frustration.

"Who is watching the kids?"

"Not you Sly!"

Somehow in my heart I tried to forgive him but I just can't seem to let it go. It's been a little over nine years since the Pricy and Sly incident. Nevertheless in my heart it feels like it just happened yesterday. Instantly I started to feel angry. I felt my mind beginning to trip.

Hurriedly I said, "I'll talk to you later."

Sly briskly replied, "Twinkle do you need anything?"

I wanted to tell him, a consistent flow of child support for Anisa would be nice. You know this dude is still hustling and sleeping with everybody. How do I know? Because I still have connects in Philly who keep me updated. Like I told you before, the hood always has the official tapes. And for those of you who don't know, you can't get child support from dudes that sell drugs or who is collecting SSI. SSI comes from the State, which is like a form of welfare and the State will not take from the State. Being that Sly never worked he cannot collect SSD. So I am out of luck. The only way I can get around that is to file a fraudulent SSI claim basically making up a lie stating that something is wrong with Anisa.

My morals will not allow me to do no foolishness like that. Anyhow back to Sly's question to me, did I need anything?

I told him that I was good and I will talk to him later. During these ten years, Sly still would come over from time to time but nothing would pop off. At times I would want to smash just because but my vow with God meant so much more to me then Sly's quick fix community... well you know.

Being human is hard at times because this thing called free will can mess you up if you allow it. Real talk one right smile and one wrong yes will have me back in the Web's mess. Is it really worth it? Hell no! But my flesh is so weak.

I constantly remind myself that in my weakness God's strength is made perfect. But God how much longer must I abstain? How much longer will I have to say no? Not only to fornication but to the lustful dreams that I have which terrorizes me in the middle of the night. Or what about the memories and recall about the love that I once had for him. At times it feels like torture.

Just because I am saved the feeling of being horny did not go away and whoever tells you that their feelings went away is a liar and they are still doing it. Sometimes I want to pop in a flick and touch myself, but again I ask myself is it worth it? The answer is no. If I entertain flesh then I will get flesh results. No good thing dwells in mine or your flesh. Sin is nasty, however it feels good and it is crafty.

It will make you think that he or she is good for you. Lust is an illusion that will deceive you, it will have you singing "Ohh La La La" but after it is all said and done you will be singing "Ohh Nah Nah" look what you just started and this time it will be seven times worse. The consequences of sin are horrific. It breaks your heart and turns you out. That thing called "dictonite" is deadly and so is your "party mix." Stop mixing with everybody at the party. Everything and everybody just don't mix.

Be mindful of who you let enter you because it will poison you. Not only will it affect your sweet pink but it will affect your soul and have you looking and thinking straight crazy or loco. Although I'm aware of this, I still felt lonely. So I went to sleep. I was awakened in the middle of the night by the phlebotomists, an eccentric yet cool transvestite. I know someone just said to their self, how did I know? I know because she told me. I'm not sure why she told me, perhaps she felt comfortable.

She stated, "If my blood work comes back okay it will be a strong possibility, I will get discharged later today."

I was glad about that. The entire time I was in the hospital I didn't watch TV. I just prayed. The Lord told me that before I go home. I had to let go of all of the hurt, forgive myself and forgive everyone who hurt me.

My internal hurt was now beginning to affect me physiologically; the pain was weakening my immune system, which comes from the root of a broken spirit and broken heart. God commanded me to announce these spirits to come up and out of me and for me to leave it here. For years I've held my junk and other people's junk inside. Is it worth it? No! The reality is the people who hurt me is doing them and probably excited that I'm here.

People will try to drive you insane. Individuals that are in bondage want you to remain there with them; bitter people, people that have a heart of flint, and haters are all in bondage.

I decided to be free and not care about what people think about me. No one has the ability to give me life, no one wakes me up in the morning and no one but God watches and protects me when I'm sleeping. I desire a good and happy life. My life is what I make it.

For now on I'm going to be real with my feelings say what's on my mind respectfully and then chuck up my deuces. I am almost forty still dealing with the same ish and the same people. Come on! Something has to give.

I said my prayer and promised God that I'm leaving all of this crap here in this hospital. Around mid-morning the Registered Nurse stated the doctor will be in to discuss my blood results shortly. While waiting I kept saying, "I'm new and I don't care who likes it or not. God gave me permission to let it go." I washed, got myself together and told myself that no longer will I wear this raggedy wig. It just didn't make any sense to wear a wig when I have all of this thick and long hair on my head.

The Doctor entered my room at 2:15 p.m. she said, "Lisa you look beautiful."

"Thank you, but I'm not going to look so beautiful if you don't tell me what I want to hear," followed by a devious smirk.

"Your white blood cells are still elevated however; they are decreasing which is a good thing."

So quickly, I responded, "Does that mean I'm going home?"

She smiled and replied, "Yes."

Before she left the room she looked at me with a demanding yet caring look and stated, "Lisa take care of yourself."

"I'm going to do my best Doc."

She gave me instructions and prescriptions to fill, and then told me, "I was free to leave."

I called Shaquan, and asked him to come and get me because I've just been discharged. While waiting for him, I packed my bags, took all of the smell goods and socks which they gave me, then sat on my bed with a goofy big smile on my face.

Shaquan walks in and gave me a kiss on my cheek, "Mom let's be out."

"You ain't say nothing but a word son."

As we were walking out of the room the male nurse asked me if I wanted him to wheel me downstairs in a wheel chair. I looked at him like dude go somewhere, however I mustered up a slight smile and replied, "No thank you." Shaquan looked at me while shaking his head and babbled, "Mom they wildin' here."

"I know right."

When we entered the elevator I felt like this was the beginning of a new day and new journey. The sun was very bright as we walked outside and it was uncomfortably hot. Shaquan took me to get my prescription filled. I asked him to take me to the beauty supply store.

I purchased black hair dye, a ponytail, and then got my eyebrows arched. The ponytail was just going to hold me over until I could make a hair appointment. Like I previously told you, I made up my mind not to wear wigs no more. I was hungry and had a taste for Spanish food so Shaquan drove me to Freddy's in Camden.

On our way there, Anisa called me, because she just got out of school. She asked me, "Did I get released from the hospital?"

"Honeybun yes, your brother and I are on our way to Freddy's we'll be home soon."

Anisa was hyped I was coming home, and with good food. As my son was driving and blasting his music I asked him to turn it down. I expressed to him that I was very proud of him.

"Why Mom?"

"Son you are seventeen years old a senior and never had a father around. The streets tried to grip you up, family members tried to build a wedge between us and no matter what you always had my back, respected me and obeyed me. After all, it means a lot to a single mother raising a son.

I made many mistakes with you especially you being the eldest child. Although I was young when I had you, our mother and son bond still remains strong which I am very thankful."

While cruzin' in the car we were jamming. I was reminded how I used to bump my music when I was his age and real talk I still do. Turn down for what! You know what I'm saying. We got to Freddy's ordered and left.

On the way home my son was driving so fast, I encouraged him to slow down. As I told him to slow down a text message came through on his phone when he looked down at the phone he ran a red light.

"Jesus!" I screamed because a car was right in front of us, my life flashed in front of me. Shaquan swerved and just missed the car. My God! I gave him the evil eye.

Shaquan said in a cool tone, "My bad Mom."

Now yelling, 'my bad' I continued, "What is bad is the fact you're driving 100 miles per hour, you have nowhere to go and furthermore you are an inexperienced driver. What's bad is; you could have killed someone or me because you're driving like a bat out of hell. If you want to kill yourself that is your issue but I want to live."

"Mom chill."

"You chill," I said aggressively as I rolled my eyes. My nerves were bad and the energy was off for the remainder of the ride. I couldn't wait to get home so I could just relax. Finally we arrived at my house safe and sound. Anisa greeted me with a hug and gave her brother a hug. Anisa noticed the disgusted look on my face.

"Mommy what's wrong."

"Your brother almost killed me, himself and somebody else."

Shaquan interjected, "Alright Mom and Anisa love y'all and I'll talk to y'all later."

Anisa gave her brother another hug. I hollered see you later. As we ate Anisa communicated to me about her stay when she was with her Grandparents. While Anisa was there she cooked and helped my Mom with chores. Although Anisa is ten she cooks and cleans like she is twenty-five years old, she loves to cook and clean.

Her dad called while we were talking. *I was just thinking about him.*

"Hello," I answered.

"Twinkle are you still in the hospital?"

"No, I just got out."

"Where is CC?"

"Right here."

"Hey Daddy."

Sly must have asked Anisa what she was doing. Then, I heard her say, "Mommy and I are eating Spanish food." They talked for a few minutes. Then Anisa said, "Mom, Dad wants to talk to you."

"What's up Sly?"

He responded real slick, "I was just making sure my VP was good."

"Negro I am not your VP but I'm good. Are you high Sly because I sense in my spirit you are under the influence."

"Nah Twinkle, I'm not high. I called you in the spirit of concern."

"Okay Sly! I can't with you. I just got home and I'm eating, I'll talk to you later."

"Twinkle when are you going back to work?"

"Why Sly?"

"Because I want to make sure you and the kids are good."

"I'm not sure when I'm going back."

"So you not going to tell me," Sly said irritably.

"No I'm not Sly, because it is none of your business."

"This is the shit I'm talking about Twinkle," he snapped.

"Well, then hang up the phone. Sly you are really starting to aggravate me. I told you that I'm eating and you continue to ask me irrelevant questions."

"Alright! Bye then," Sly shouted.

I just hung up the phone. After the phone call ended, Anisa asked, "Mommy why do you and Daddy still argue?"

"Honeybun if I knew the answer your father and I would be the best of friends."

"Daddy told me to tell you he loves you."

I acted like I didn't hear her, because I didn't want to respond. Redirecting the conversation, "Anisa do you have homework?"

"No mommy, but I do have a science project due in a couple of weeks."

"Okay, I will get the supplies this weekend."

After we ate, I showed her my ponytail and confessed; I'm not wearing my wigs anymore.

"Thank God, Mommy, I can't stand those things anyway." I snickered.

"Mommy just do your hair."

"You just do your hair," teasingly I responded. I continued, "Why do you think I purchased this ponytail? It's not because I'm putting it in your hair."

"Mommy you are funny."

"So are you," we laughed.

We watched TV for a little while, as her bedtime approached. I reminded her to pick out her clothes for school tomorrow, afterwards wash up and brush your teeth because in about an hour you will be going to bed. While Anisa was getting ready my doorbell rang.

Chapter 2
Unspoken Words

I looked through the peephole and asked who is it? The man responded FedEx.

When I opened the door, this fine, tall; medium built, clean; caramel complexion man with high cheekbones and distinctive light brown eyes was standing in front of me. He was so fine that you would want to stalk him.

I call those types of men, "stalker(ish) fine."

I asked, "May I help you?"

"I have a package for you that you have to sign for."

Just when I was about to sign off, I noticed the address was not mine.

"Sir you are at the wrong address. The person you are looking for lives upstairs."

"Sorry Ma'am."

"No problem."

He smiled.

Being flirtatious I winked and said, "Have a good evening."

As I closed the door the song by Mary J. Blige – (Never Been) popped up in my head. I started singing "I never knew it felt like this. I never knew. (An' I never knew) I never knew you'd love like this." I was open because he was stalker(ish) fine. I don't know if my medicine had me feeling some type of way but all I know he was fine with a legit job.

After I shut the door, Anisa asked, "Who was that Mommy?"

I told her the FedEx guy had the wrong address. I finally tucked her in, we prayed and lights went out.

While I was watching TV, I started to think how bored I'm going to be tomorrow because I had not been cleared to go back to work. I decided I would do my hair tomorrow to kill sometime.

The next day, I woke Anisa up, fixed her breakfast and walked her to her bus stop. When the bus came I gave her a hug and kiss. I said to her, "Have a wonderful day." As I was walking back to my crib I saw the FedEx truck parked across the street but I didn't see ole' boy! You know I was looking for his fine self.

Around noon, I started to color my hair while pumpin' my music. I was in my zone. I heard my doorbell ringing; it was as if someone kept constantly pushing the doorbell. I started to get agitated. *Who is at my darn door?*

Can I just spend some time to myself? Furthermore when I'm doing my hair I do not like to be disturbed.

I peeped through the peephole. O shoot! It's the FedEx guy. My hair is a mess, I wanted to answer the door so bad but my pride would not allow me to do so. Dang! But I do want his number.

Nah! He can't see me like this. I just ignored the door and continued coloring my hair. I was so mad at myself and now questions of curiosity started to arise. What could he possibly want? Why is he at my door? It's been ten years and I haven't dated anyone.

Well I dated a few cats from the church but real talk they were no better than Sly. The reality of it is, when you tell guys that you are waiting for marriage they are not trying to hear it.

It's a shame church girls have a reputation of being the biggest freaks. Just because you go to church doesn't make you delivered it just simply means, that you go to church, nothing more and nothing less.

Now I'm done my hair and my doorbell rings again. Instantly I got excited because I just knew it was the FedEx guy. I said out loud, perfect timing Heavenly Father, thank you for not allowing me to miss my opportunity. Good look.

I opened the door with a smile on my face. To my unfortunate surprise it was Sly.

"What do you want Sly?" I asked with an attitude of disappointment.

"Baby Mom, I was checking on you and got you some groceries, Ginger Ale and soup."

Now sighing, "Did I ask you for any groceries?"

"I was in the area Twinkle and decided to come through."

"Really Sly! The area! How does one cross the Betsy Ross Bridge and be in my area?"

"Twinkle, are you going to let me in?"

"Come on." I gave him the cold shoulder.

"How are you feeling?"

"I'm doing better."

"You look cute."

"Thanks Sly," I responded being short.

Sly put the groceries in the kitchen and asked was I expecting company?

I uttered, "If I was, what would it of mattered. You are here, why didn't you call me?"

"I wanted to surprise you Twinkle."

"Sly no you didn't, you are here because you are being nosey. Sly where is your girl? Or should I say your host of women."

"You're my girl," Sly hastily responded.

"Oh yeah, I am, because I'm the only person here. Whatever Sly! What do you want?"

"I want a hug Twinkle."

Although I was reluctant I gave him a hug. Sly held me so tight.

"Twinkle I miss you and I don't know what I would do if something happened to you."

"Nothing is going to happen to me."

"You smell so good."

"Sly back up off me. I don't know where you just went in your mind, but I'm not going there with you."

But straight talk in my mind I was like boy you better back up because I'm about to jump all over you. My flesh was weak. That darn Sly had the mojo with his mean looking self. Sly peeped it. After being with and around someone for years there is an energy I call 'unspoken words.' The "unspoken words" have a language that Sly and I understood all too well.

"Keep it real Twinkle, you miss me."

"No I don't Sly."

Sly insisted, "Yes you do."

"No I don't. The only thing I miss is your cooking."

Sly kissed me on the forehead, "I'm sorry Twinkle for everything, and I miss you."

I responded, "I know you are and I know you do." I continued; "If you think you're going to get some you might as well leave now. If we haven't got back together in nine years we are definitely not getting back together now."

"Why not," Sly exclaimed!

"It's not meant, I don't believe in going backwards looking back gets you / me nowhere."

"Twinkle you're not going backwards, you will be moving forward."

"How's that Sly?"

"I am a changed man," Sly said with confidence.

"Oh really, How are you a changed man?"

"VP, I gave up the game and I got a job doing demolition."

"Well, where are my child support checks?"

"I work under the table, but it's legit."

"Sly it's not legit. You have not changed; you just admitted you work under the table. How is under the table legit? I'll tell you the answer Sly. It's not."

"VP, come here, sit on my lap and relax. I didn't come here to upset you. Here is five hundred dollars for CC this is the real reason why I came over. I won some money playing numbers at the number house."

"Didn't you just tell me you are legit?"

"I am Twinkle, I don't hustle no more."

"Playing numbers at the number house is illegal."

"Why Twinkle, when playing the lottery is legal?"

"Sly because it is!" Sly started kissing me.

At first I was resisting him; I kept moving my face away from him telling him to stop. After a while, I gave in and started kissing him back. He whispered, "Twinkle if my thing gets hard you are going to give me some."

Like a flash I gave away out of the lust zone and hopped off his lap. It's been nine years of being celibate, am I ever going to get delivered from the Spirit of lust? God I need your help. These feelings are natural, however being perverted is unnatural.

My flesh wants a fix; although I know it's wrong how long can I continue to hold on. Sly is here and I know he knows this look in my eyes. Even though I try to hide it he knows it's a lie. I know in my heart Mr. Wrong will compromise my purity and then disappear. But Mr. Right will wait on my purity and also change my last name.

Is there really a Mr. Right? And if it is then where is he? Is it the FedEx guy? I'm so tired of waiting. I didn't know when I said yes to you God that I would have to suffer loneliness, and continue to say no to what I really want to do. I definitely didn't know I would still have feelings for Sly. My heart does not love Sly but my flesh misses him. Lord help me to hold out, I need your help to remain willing and obedient.

The old folks used to say just take a cold shower. I have taken thousands of cold showers and it doesn't work

Jesus. Denying my flesh feels like torture but corrupting my spirit is death. I must think of those things, which are lovely and pure. But how can I when I live in a perverse world? I always keep in mind, one right smile and one wrong yes and I will be back a mess. Is it worth my salvation? Heaven no!

While Sly sat on one side of the couch I sat on the other. These were the "unspoken words" racing through my mind.

Sly breaking the silence, "Twinkle are you alright?"

"Yes!"

"What type of medicine are you taking?"

"Why Sly?"

"You seem like your mind is somewhere else."

"My mind is somewhere else," I answered.

Sly jestingly responded, "Twinkle get your mind right."

"Sly my mind is not right because you are not right and you being here is a distraction."

"Twinkle I came in peace."

"Okay! Thank you and now you can leave in peace Sly."

"I can't stay until my daughter gets home from school?"

I glanced at Sly like you are so full of it.

Sly responded, "Thanks Twinkle."

While Sly waited he started to make some homemade chicken and rice soup. He cleaned the chicken put water in the pot. Cut up some garlic, celery and onion and let it all cook with the chicken.

Soon the food started to smell good. Real good! Before you knew it the food was done and Anisa was walking in the door. When Anisa saw her dad, she looked at me as if she was saying why is dad here?

Sly said, "What's up CC."

"Hey Dad," She walked over to him while he was sitting on the couch and gave him a hug.

I asked, "Anisa how was school?"

"Mommy it was okay. This girl was teasing me saying I was wearing Bans instead of Vans." Anisa continued to say, "This girl is so corny, and she had the courage to say 'no shade no tea Hun.'

Mom I looked at her and said, "That's why you are banned with your bootleg chucks on your feet. Bye girl!" And I walked away.

Sly and I started laughing; then he said, "You are just like mom with that smart ass mouth." Anisa ignored him.

"CC I made you and your mom some chicken soup and rice."

"Thanks Dad but it is the middle of May. I'm okay, I'll just eat a turkey and cheese sandwich."

Sly responded, "I got some hamburger meat. Do you want me to make you some Tacos for dinner?"

With much excitement Anisa shouted, "Yes Daddy!"

This dude needs to go home. Now he is making more food. So this means his stay is going to be prolonged. Just go home already. Ugh!

"Mommy I'm going to do my homework in my room."

"Okay Baby."

While Sly was preparing to cook the tacos, he declared, "Twinkle we are family and we should try to make it work again."

Being nice nasty asked, "Why should we do that Sly."

"I love you, Shaquan and CC. I belong here doing my fatherly duties."

"Sly! Fatherly duties, Umm! What is your definition of fatherly duties?"

"Working and helping you take care of the kids."

"Guess what Sly; we don't have to be together for

you to do that. You don't even do your "fatherly duties" on a consistent basis now. So how in the world are you suddenly going to be unfailing?" *Sly is looking appalled.* I continued, "You are not even faithful over a few things, so you will definitely not be faithful to more commitment and responsibility.

How about this Sly! Get a legit job, work there steady for at least one year. Stop drinking and smoking weed, purchase a house and be celibate with me and maybe we can revisit this conversation."

Speedily Sly replied, "I am celibate."

"No you are not Sly, you sell-a-bit. Of only the Lord knows what."

Sly getting agitated responded, "Whatever Twinkle, I'm never going to be good enough for you.

If I'm not kissing your ass then you are never going to be satisfied. You don't even appreciate the fact I'm here checking on you."

"Sly you are only checking up on me for your own manipulative motives. You being here isn't genuine. Who do you think you are fooling? You over here cooking and giving Anisa five hundred dollars whenever you feel like it, is nothing special. How about being a dependable father. Spend time with her and help her with her homework.

Go watch her cheerlead at her games. Go to parent teacher conferences with me for Christ sake. Call her on a regular and when she calls you pick up the damn phone.

But instead you make up lame excuses and come and go as you please. You feel when you pop up, we are supposed to treat you like a king from "Coming to America" and get the baskets full of flower petals and throw them down whenever you walk and chant "All praises to Sly."

I'm not ever going to make you feel special because what you are doing is what you are supposed to do chump. You don't get any free- b's here. You are only here because I made the initiative and called you while I was in the hospital and your deceitful spirit peeped I was vulnerable.

You sniffed a possible opportunity to get me open again. Just so you can hurt me like you always do and did. The season of me being delusional is over."

"Twinkle I don't want to hear this shit."

I was about to keep going but I quickly remembered that he didn't give Anisa the money yet. So I humbled myself instantly and said, "Bae' this medicine got me trippin'. I really appreciate you being here fixing me soup and making Anisa tacos.

My body is just reacting weird to this medicine." *Look y'all I need the five hundred dollars so I'm going to bite the bullet.* Sly forcefully responded, "Do you want me to leave?" In my high-pitched whiny voice I replied, "No baby you know that I miss you and I'm glad that you are here."

Then shut up take a selfie and give me a kiss.

"Sly my mouth is dry and hot from these meds."

"Well eat something to change the taste in your mouth."

"What you trying to be funny Sly?" I gave him a kiss on the cheek and said, "Thanks baby."

Anisa walked into the living room and asked, "Is the food almost done."

Sly responded, "Yes CC, give it a few minutes."

Anisa being persistent replied, "Hurry it up Dad because it smells good up in here."

Sly gave her a little smile. Sly demanded I taste the soup and tell him how I like it.

"I'm going to wait until the tacos are done so we all can eat together. There is no need for me to taste test the soup, I know you hooked it up."

My attitude with Sly left the building. Child I was thinking about all of the things Anisa and I was going to do with the five hundred dollars.

Clearly, the thought of money changed my mind and my attitude. The food was finally done, while I was eating I made sure to boost Sly's ego by telling him how good the soup is.

"Twinkle that soup is going to make you feel much better."

"Dad these tacos are bangin'."

"CC, I'm glad you are enjoying them."

I hope by me stroking Sly's ego he will give me five hundred more dollars in a couple of weeks.

Sometimes you got to get in where you fit in. See, Sly likes to feel needed and he likes to feel as if he is in control. Co- dependency is another form of an ungodly soul tie. People that suffer from this issue are manipulative and play a lot of mind games because they try to make you feel like you need them.

Often times these people deal with insecurity issues. These individuals truly believe you will not be able to survive or do anything without them. Somewhere in there mind they believe they are "god," they also believe they created you along with thinking they have the power to make and break you.

I simply laugh at these people. Co- dependent individuals all say the same line which is, "they are going to need me before I need them." What mind boggles me, is they really believe that foolery. These people don't have the knowledge to understand, without God's power you can't do anything.

Listen, the only person you need is God. He will orchestrate the people in your life to help you with pure motives, without the headache.

Always remember this: If you have to beg anyone to do anything for you then it is not God. Just wait, God will come through for you in his time.

After we ate, I reviewed Anisa's homework, she didn't like doing her homework, but she did it. Despite her not liking to do her homework it was done and done correctly.

Around 8:30p.m. I told Anisa to start getting ready to go to bed. She picked her clothes out, washed up and brushed her teeth. I wanted to ask Sly so bad what time are you leaving and when are you going to give Anisa the money.

This is what I'm talking about, people who like control is a nuisance. They just do things with the wrong intent in hoping somewhere down the line there counterfeit act will eventually benefit them.

When someone does something nice for you and expect something in return that is not being kind that is called being manipulative and running game. Sly purposely was waiting until the last minute to give Anisa her money so he can lengthen his stay. I started to get pissed off so I finally asked Sly when was he going to give Anisa the money. Being facetious I followed up with tomorrow!!!

Sly responded, "Twinkle I'm going to give her the money before she goes to bed."

"Sly she is getting ready now, what you going to tuck the money under her pillow like you are the tooth fairy?"

"Twinkle you are always getting smart."

"I'm not getting smart, I'm serious," I grunted while frowning at him. While Sly and I were talking Anisa was picking out her clothes but me knowing my daughter she was ear hustling.

"CC!" Sly called her.

"Yes Daddy," she said while walking into the living room.

"Daddy just wants you to know that I'm proud of you and I love you."

CC, smiled and replied, "Daddy I love you too."

Here is some money for you, tell your mom to buy you some cute clothes for the summer. Buy yourself some new sneakers and some outfits.

"Thanks Daddy."

"I'm giving you 5 beans which is five hundred dollars, don't spend it all in one place."

"Okay Dad I won't", she assured with a cheerful smile. "Daddy you are always full of surprises."

I co-signed, "Yes your dad is." Just then Shaquan walked into the house from work.

My son was so handsome and hardworking. He would go to school, after school he would go to track practice and from there he would go to work. He worked at Shoprite from 6pm – 8:45pm. I was so proud of him.

"What's up Sly?" They gave each other daps.

"Your Mom told me you had to work today."

"No, I didn't Sly, you always lying."

Shaquan chuckled a little. "Mom today was crazy. I saw a man trying to rob an old lady in the parking lot of Shoprite. While I was outside pushing carts for some reason I was watching this old lady walk. Out of nowhere I noticed some guy trying to grab her purse."

I shouted, "Yo! Yo!"

When I started to run towards him, some of my co-workers followed me. The guy started running and I caught him, grabbed him and took him down. Come to find out it, was my ole' head from school. This dude was screaming 'young buck let me go.' I was going to, because he looked out for me back in the day when I was about to get jumped.

By then the cops had come and arrested him. Mom come to find out, he is on that stuff."

Facetiously, I responded, "He's in love with the CoCo."

"Mom, how do you know those lyrics?"

"Son, I work with kids all day in Camden." Shaquan continued, "I don't know who I feel worse for, my ole' head or the old lady?"

"Shaquan you did the right thing," I assured. I kept speaking, "It's just messed up that you knew him."

Shaquan responded, "Wow life is crazy. I wonder what happened to him and why he chose this path to rob old ladies?"

Sly chimed in, "That's not cool though, because if someone tries to rob my mom. It's going to be something foreal, foreal," he said while nodding his head.

I interjected, "By the time you would find out, the guy would be caught and in jail. You are Casper the friendly ghost, first cousin Dasper the meanly ghost, you disappear."

Sly changing the subject, "Shaquan I made some chicken soup and tacos."

Shaquan responded, "That what's up." Shaquan washed his hands and started to make a taco.

Sly said, "Twinkle I'm about to be out."

"Okay! I'll see you later."

Sly walked over to Anisa. "Give your dad a kiss I'm about to leave."

Before Sly left, he decided to take the trash out. Sly asked Shaquan to walk him to the dumpster. They went outside, who knows what Sly was up to because he is always scheming. I tucked Anisa into bed and said our prayers.

"Mommy; I can't wait to go shopping." Her eyes got bright.

Happily I responded, "I can't wait neither. Now we can get your supplies for your project." In unison said, "then we can go shopping." We said in our Keenen and Marlon Wayans voice from the movie "White Chicks."

We hugged; I told her goodnight and sweet dreams. I started to straighten the kitchen. I noticed that Shaquan been outside for about fifteen minutes with Sly.

I wondered what they are talking about. Eventually, Shaquan came back in with a smile on his face. "Mom, Sly gave me two hundred and fifty dollars and instructed me to give you four hundred dollars."

"Oh! He must be ballin' he must have hit the number real good at the number house."

"Mom! What is the number house?"

"It's a house where they illegally play numbers, gamble and other illegal activity."

"Wow! The boy Sly," Shaquan said while shaking his head. "It's never a dull moment with him." He continued, "That's your man Mom."

"No he is not my man he is Anisa's father that's all and that is it."

Chapter 3

Confessions

"Mom I haven't seen my Dad since I was five. Do you know where he is? I'm about to graduate from high school and I would like to talk to him and possibly see him."

"Son, I hesitated never mind."

I've been holding a secret from Shaquan since he was five and didn't know how to tell him.

"Mom, are you okay?"

"Yes, I am. These meds have me zoning in and out."

I changed the subject. "How was track practice?"

"It was good, but I'm a little sore though." Shaquan told me he was running so fast that his coach said that he looked like a runaway slave.

"Mom I didn't know if I should have taken the statement personal or not, being that he is Caucasian."

"Son, I'm sure your coach didn't mean any harm."

"But why did he have to compare me to a slave?"

"Shaquan I don't know, your overthinking. It's really not that serious."

"Mom these tacos are hitting for something."

"Yeah you know Sly; you can always count on him for a good meal," I replied.

"Son, I'm tired, I'm about to take it down. Love you."

"Love you too."

I went into my room; prayed and asked God to give me the wisdom on how to tell my son this secret I've been holding on to for so many years.

Heavenly Father, I've did things in my past I'm not proud about nor was it pleasing to you. Although, I am saved I still struggle with a lot of things, but I can't continue to live a lie. The word of God states the truth will make you free. I'm so ashamed; I would let this secret tarry for so long.

What is my son going to say and think about me? I love my son so much and he has a good head on his shoulders. I don't want to hurt him but if someone else tells him before me it's going to hurt him even the more.

Give me the strength and the courage to tell him the truth. This secret has been lying on my heart for entirely too long and I must release it. I pray this will not come in between us. I also pray my son and I will remain close in Jesus Name Amen.

I drifted off to sleep. The next morning Anisa and Shaquan got ready for school. The morning really went smooth everyone woke up on time and there was no bickering. Diamond called me early morning to check up on me.

"Hey sis," I answered.

"Yo! Sis what's poppin'?"

Nothing just chilling, Sly came through yesterday fixed me some soup and fixed the kids tacos.

Diamond blurted, "Chef *sorry* is always cooking you these meals. He is always doing something slick," she continued, "Did you give him some?"

"Some of what Diamond?"

"That berry balsamic," she said in her ghetto voice.

"No, it's not even like that sis. You already know what it is."

"I know Twinkle, but mistakes happen."

"I hear you Diamond, but not on my watch. Sly gave me a few dollars."

"Word sis!"

"Word! Do you need a couple of dollars?"

"You darn right I never turn down money."

"When are you coming through?"

"I'm coming now Twinkle."

"Diamond, you didn't go to work?"

"No, I took off, because I had to take care of some things."

"Alright cool. This works out for me so when I call Sly and thank him, he won't feel compelled to come through because you will be here."

"Sis real talk, why does Sly feel comfortable to pop up at your house?" She continued, "You ain't been with him in how long? You need to check him. What's going to happen when you start dating again? Your man ain't going to tolerate that bull. No real dude is going to go for it and Sly is not worth arguing about."

"Diamond just bring your behind over and don't take all day, because you know how you get lost."

"I'll be there."

"What time Diamond?"

"Dang sis why are you clockin' me? It ain't like you are going somewhere."

"I don't care. Diamond what if I decide to go out."

Diamond in fun responded, "Stop getting yourself all worked up. I'll be there around noon."

"Around noon," I replied while mocking her. "Sis, you are speaking to me, not one of your colleagues." We both laughed. "Okay, I said I will see you then."

After we hung up I thought to myself I should call Sly and thank him for the money. Although I didn't want to,

I figured it wasn't going to hurt to be nice. It's nice to be nice at times.

I dialed his number, the phone rang and his voicemail picked up. I hung up because I don't like leaving messages. He will call me back, when he realizes he has a missed call.

A few minutes later the phone rung and it was Sly.

I answered, "Hey!"

The voice on the other end responded, "*Hellah, Hellah, Hellah...*"

Really, it is never ending with Sly. The female asked, "Who dis?"

"You called my phone," I implied and ask her, "Who's this?"

"This is Sharon, Sly's baby mom," she said with a not so pleasing tone.

"Okay, this is Twinkle is Sly there?"

"No he just stepped out and left his phone here."

"When he gets back in can you ask him to call me?"

"Is this Anisa's mom?"

"Yes."

"Did Sly tell you that we were F-in since your daughter was four months old? We also have a daughter together."

"No!"

"Our daughter is eight and her name is Sha'ranay."

"Congratulations Sharon."

"Are you and Sly still messing around?"

"Do me a favor, when Sly comes back ask him."

"Twinkle why are you calling my man?"

"Because I can, enjoy your day Sharon and then I banged on her."

I was so angry, because Anisa is ten years old. Which means the chick I was talking to, obviously was messing with Sly when we were together. That scumbag! He never told me he had more kids after Anisa. You know what, why am I surprised?

This has always been Sly's M/O. Lie, smash, lie again and smash some more. This clown never stops. You can't put a crown on a clown and expect him to act like a king.

I wanted to call back and tell her off. But I asked myself why would I do that? I haven't messed with Sly in nine years and thank God I have not, if I did I would be so hurt right now.

God I said, yelling. "Thank you so much for being a keeper. Thank you so much for giving me the strength to say no and although I'm by myself I have peace of mind."

I wonder how many more kids Sly had when we were together. I got myself together before my sister came over. I watched TV and relaxed. I wasn't hundred percent well from the pneumonia, I still was getting shortness of breath and from time to time I was running slight fevers.

Midafternoon my sis knocks on the door.

"Hey sis," I said as I opened the door.

"What's up?" Diamond walked in and sat down.

I asked her did she want something to eat.

"What do you have Twinkle."

"I have soup and tacos."

"Do you have any tortillas?"

"Yes, why?"

"I'm going to make a taco salad."

"Okay, help yourself."

While Diamond was making her taco salad, I said, "Let me tell you about the malarkey that just happened. Why did I call Sly and his baby mom Sharon called me back telling me her and Sly have an eight year-old daughter."

"Word sis!"

"Word is bond!"

Diamond questioned, "Are you surprised? We all know he believes in being fruitful and multiplying just like those nasty roaches do." We chuckled, "Diamond this dude stay in drama."

"He always messes up your Feng Shui Twinkle." She continued, "You need to hit him with a left and a right and tell him bye boy foreal."

"I'm so glad I didn't smash him, because this conversation would have gone another way."

Diamond responded, "I know you would have been in Philly right now cussing the chick out and literally hitting Sly with a right and left. Sick and all you would have not cared."

"Thank God for deliverance," I replied.

"God had to save you Twinkle because it is just better for the world. Now don't get me wrong you are still crazy, it's just justified."

"Diamond you are hilarious."

"I'm being real. I'm guessing Sly didn't call you back?"

"No, but he will in a few days after he get his lie together."

Diamond responded, "Sly needs Jesus, a therapist and an honest hug." We laughed some more.

Diamond changing the subject asked, "Have you spoken to Kay?"

"No ever since I got saved she's been acting funny."

"Wow sis!"

"I know Diamond we were cool since we were wearing pigtails and burets. It hurts because no matter what I really love Kay like a sis."

"What happened?" Diamond asked being concerned?

"Remember when I got saved Kay, Ree, C and Bertha started going to church as well. Although we went to different churches it didn't matter because we were still family."

Diamond interjected, "You know at times family is the first to hurt you."

"Literally, Kay started getting hungry for money because she had lost her job at the bank. Not sure why she got fired but she did. As a result she started stealing and selling the merchandise. I didn't judge her I just told her to be careful. I mean she is grown and grown people are going to do what they do.

Any who! Kay wanted more money so she started going to New York looking for strippers because she started throwing strip parties.

One day she called to invite me to one of her parties. Kay asked me to collect the money because she needed honest hands because her home-girl which was collecting the money kept stinging her. I explained to Kay I couldn't entertain that atmosphere. She went to say we are family and I should come support her hustle.

Again, I told Kay I'm not supporting, and for her to put her trust in God. But she wasn't trying to hear it. Kay confessed she was really thirsty because her bills were very delinquent. I expressed I understand however, the only thing I will be collecting is an offering."

Kay replied, "I see where your loyalty stands. You used to be my partner in crime."

"I articulated to Kay I switched partners and now I'm your partner in Christ and this is the only way for me. I still got love for you but I love God much more. I explained to Kay this was a set up from the enemy and if she keeps entertaining the devil he is going to make a fool out of her."

Kay responded, "Whatever and I'm going to get this money at all cost."

I wished her well and ended the phone call. "Sis, you feel me? I'm not going back. I won too many battles to go back."

Diamond, responded, "I feel you."

"Then one day I saw her at the market." I said, "Hey girl!" Kay gave me a fake hi and a half wave.

"Diamond you know I kiss nobody's behind. You know my motto, "mother had you and mother… well you fill in the blank."

Diamond, changing the subject. "I saw Ree at the dollar store and she was turned up and so was I."

"Yeah," I responded, "Ree and I don't speak neither; you remember she became an ordained minister?"

"Yeah Sis! That's why it took me off guard when I saw her turned up."

Ree started distancing herself from me because she started drinking and smoking weed again. One day Ree called me to come by to chill with her. So I did. Of course she had her drinks; while we were talking she was drinking. Ree asked me did I want anything to drink. I told her I was good.

However, I did tell her I wanted some of the Stuffed shells she made. So while she drank, I ate. Now Ree feeling the liquor said, "Twinkle lets drive to Philly and go to the bar where Sly is?"

I asked her, "Why?"

Ree responded, "To start some shit with him."

I told Ree I'm not going to Philly to sit in the same bar as Sly especially because I don't drink.

Ree responded sarcastically, "Then order a soda."

I asked Ree, "Do you hear what you are saying. That does not make any sense."

Diamond, remember back in the day when I used to smoke weed everybody knew I did not do shot guns. One time we were over Sly's house smoking and Ree asked Sly could he give her a shotgun. Ree knew Sly was going to say yes. While he was giving her the shot gun, Ree got so close to his mouth that Sly backed up and shouted, "Yo Twinkle! Your girl is trying to kiss me."

 When I asked her about it, Ree replied, "She wasn't trying to kiss Sly." I overlooked it.

"Now years later, Ree is asking for us to drive to Philly to start some unnecessary drama with Sly. My question is why don't we drive to Burlington city and start some stuff with Nap at the bar. That's who she needs to be thinking about, not my baby dad.

That was shade; you know when people start drinking they get real loose with their mouth. That's why the Bible states to be sober minded, after that evening, Ree put a bad taste in my mouth.

Then months later I went to the VFW in Willingboro, because Leslie from the church works and cooks in the kitchen. I had a taste for her fried shrimp, chicken wings and cheesy crab fries. I ordered my food, and when I went in to pick up my food. Guess who was sitting at the bar getting turned up. I spoke to Ree, but she acted like she didn't see or hear me. So, I walked into the kitchen got my food and left.

Anisa was in the car waiting for me. Sis! I was still cool. But this chick was on some secret vindictive type ish. Ree saw Shaquan at Yani's nephew birthday party and had the nerve to tell Shaquan, "Your mom be at the bar." Making it seem like I was bustin' it up in there.

Diamond interjected, "I'm not surprised. Ree has always been a liar. I was never feeling her from day one. She never sat right with me."

Shaquan started questioning me asking me was I drinking. I told him, "No and asked him why." At the time Shaquan didn't tell me why he asked the question. Afterwards, I didn't think twice about it. Honestly I thought he was asking me because he was drinking from time to time.

The truth came out three months later when Anisa and I went to get our nails and eyebrows done. Anisa and I saw Ree at the Salon, I said what's up to her and Anisa waved at her. Ree waved back and said no more. Well this chick saw Shaquan while he was driving and this chick goes out of her way to tell him to pull over.

When Shaquan pulled over, Ree shared seeing Anisa and me at the nail salon. When Anisa waved at her, she told him that I smacked Anisa's hand and told Anisa that we don't speak to her anymore. Shaquan secretly asked Anisa first. After Anisa told him that was not true, it was then that Shaquan told me that Ree told him about me being in the bar.

After Shaquan told me this I went right to Ree's mom house thinking that she still lived there. I needed to ask her what is the problem and why is she constantly lying on me to my son.

Diamond being humorous said, "You know liars enjoy drama." She continued, "Ree probably wanted a reaction from you just so your name could be in her mouth." I replied, "She was about to get a reaction she was not prepared for." We laughed.

Anyway I explained to her mom what was going on and stated if Ree wants to talk to me about something then she can. I was trying to give Ree the benefit of doubt because I really didn't want any bad blood between us. It was then that Ree's mom explained to me she moved, however her mom told me she still had love for me and she would definitely relay the message.

I told her thank you and gave her a hug good bye.

"Dag Sis!" Diamond shouted, "Those chicks stabbed you in the back and probably telling everyone that they're bleeding."

"Sis, you know I don't care. They are shifty and I shifted out of their lives. My atmosphere is a no negative zone."

Diamond being hesitant, "I almost don't want to ask you about C and Bertha."

"Bertha moved to Arizona we are still cool. However, I cut C off."

"OMG?" Diamond being surprised? "What did sweet C do?"

"C meant this guy online and was meeting him in Ocean County I think she needed someone to talk to. Now she told me they were only friends, which I kind of believed her."

Diamond being jocular, "Okay sis believe that if you want too."

I smirked. "However, the problem was she told T-Bone she was meeting the guy along with telling him I was watching Joshua when she would go on her rendezvous. Why would C tell T- Bone that?"

Diamond responded, "To make him jealous, C like that craziness. That's why she continued to stay with him. C acts all innocent but I think at times she provokes T-Bone for attention."

"I don't know Diamond. But this dude requested me as a friend under the fictitious name Faith Hill. I thought this Faith girl was a real female. Well this dude was in boxing me like every other day acting like he was a girl named Faith sounding senseless and quoting scriptures. I started not to feel her so I started to ignore the inbox messages not even knowing that it was T-Bone.

Then one day he inboxes me going off, saying I thought you was real. He continued, "I've been with C all of these years and she told me you were the one watching our son when she was creeping with the guy she meant online."

Sis, I didn't even entertain it. I told him to leave me alone and go take care of your son.

Immediately, I called C and told her T-Bone was my Facebook friend under the name Faith Hill. C responded she knew. I asked her why she didn't tell me. She responded that she forgot. I voiced to her he was in boxing me and at first I just thought it was a looney female, not knowing it was him.

Finally I asked her why she told T-Bone I was watching Joshua when she would meet up with her friend. She denied that. Then I asked her how did he know about her meeting up with the guy? C stated that she didn't know.

Diamond you know how I don't like being lied on or lie too so I decided to leave her alone. I don't have time nor am I going to entertain confusion. It's a hard pill to swallow because they were my home-girls, but everybody is not going where God is taking me. And whoever is not qualified by God to be around me will not be.

Real rap sis, I really don't care what people do concerning their personal life. As long as it doesn't involve my children and me, I'm good. The reality is, God gives us all free will and we all fall short including me.

The bottom line is; I'm trying to make it in and walk the streets of gold and hop the pearly gates. Since Heaven has no pain, if I fall it won't even matter. Working out my own soul salvation is not easy. Nevertheless I'm not going to welcome or invite drama into my life. At times, God will change your circle to change your life for the better. One wrong distraction and I might miss or delay what God has for me."

Diamond said, "I feel you. Instead of singing, *Started from the Bottom Now We Here.* You will be singing, *Started from the Bottom Now We're Back."*

"Diamond you crazy!"

"Sis, I don't deny it." She continued, "A lot of foul stuff went on with you in these ten years. One great thing is that cousin Pricy went to rehab, joined a church and is still clean. Pricy loves Jesus foreal."

"Diamond, why Pricy be like Paul in the Bible? Her boldness is almost scary; she walks around Camden asking people *"Do you know him?"* She's been going hard for Jesus. Sometimes I look at her like cuz I respect your passion but calm down. You don't want to scare anybody to Jesus or away from him."

Diamond replied, "I guess she's trying to get her ex- crack head squad. She is aware some of them have good hearts however they are caught up and are too weak to kick the habit."

"True, Diamond you know she is making good money as a nanny and those kids love her."

"I know and I know Pricy loves them," Diamond said with a smile on her face.

I exclaimed, "She always loved children and her weight looks good on her. Diamond I knew it was something that I had to tell you."

Right then my phone rang it was Anisa.

I answered, "Hey! Honeybun."

"Hey Mommy, I was just calling to remind you I'm taking the late bus because I have chorus. I will be home around 3:45p.m."

"Okay! Sing your heart out."

Anisa giggled and said, "I will. Love you!"

"I love you too."

After we hung up Diamond asked me if I had anything sweet to eat in my house. "After I ate the taco salad, now I'm craving for something sweet."

"I don't have anything sweet; make yourself a peanut butter and jelly sandwich."

"Twinkle that does not go together."

"Why not! It's sweet."

Diamond replied, "I need a cupcake."

In a raised voice I responded, "Diamond who has cupcakes lying around the house? Yo you are buggin'. Go to Shoprite and buy you a cupcake."

Diamond snapped back, "I don't feel like all of that."

"Sis, I don't know what to tell you. But before I forget this fine FedEx guy came over by a mistake. He was at the wrong address. I made clear to him the people he was looking for lived upstairs, but this dude came back the next day. I didn't open the door because I was doing my hair and my pride wouldn't allow me to open the door. But I wanted to so bad."

Diamond replied, "Sis! You are always trying to be cute."

"Yes I am," I replied with a cocky attitude. I continued to say, "If it's meant to be then he will come back. Diamond the crazy thing is I saw his FedEx truck outside when I walked Anisa to the bus stop, but I didn't see him."

Diamond responded, "Sis that does not seem right."

"Why I asked?"

"Sis, take off the blonde wig." She continued, "He came to your house."

Before she could finish I rushed and reminded her he went to the wrong address.

"Okay, Twinkle I'll give him that, but you saw his truck outside she paused, but not him while you were walking Anisa to the bus stop."

"Yes," I said as I felt my face light up. "Diamond he probably lives out here."

Diamond now getting annoyed, "Twinkle when did FedEx employees start taking their company vehicles home?"

Wisecracking, I responded, "I don't know I never worked for FedEx and neither did you."

Diamond being short, "Why did he come back to your house."

"Because he was feeling your sister that's why, what you don't know." I continued, "Diamond stop hatin' on your older sis."

Diamond being humorous stated, "Oh! Maybe he is the one."

"I'm not saying all of that but he is fine with a job that's all I'm saying."

"Okay Sis!" Diamond changing the subject. "What's up with Candi?"

"The last time I spoke to Candi she was going to alcohol anonymous and she disclosed she has been clean for one hundred and twenty five days. We still talk on the phone from time to time.

However I haven't been to the Web in a while."

Diamond asked, "Why, is it because you still have feelings for Sly?"

"I miss him sometime. Honestly I think I miss the sex."

Diamond replied, "Twinkle you ain't smash in a while, it might not be what you think it is. I think that your mind is magnifying the act because you just haven't got any. Real talk if you do smash him you are definitely going to regret it.

Because unlike me you can't smash with no strings attached. You are going to want him over, want him involved with the kids. And before you know it, you will be putting dead possum's at his door. Sly is not worth it, you just found out he has an eight year old daughter. What else will you find out if you decide to be back involved in his host off women circle? It's just too much, not for only you but for the kids. Shaquan is graduating this year and he is doing well."

I chimed in, "Speaking about Shaquan he asked about his Dad. You know the last time Shaquan saw him he was five years old."

Diamond being curious asked, "Do you know where he is?"

I hesitated to answer, "Yes I know where he is. I paused, I think I know.

"Where is he?" Diamond asked. She looked at me and said sister, "You have a dirty little secret."

A look of guilt fell upon my face.

"Sis Word! You do have a secret."

Now Diamond is all excited, "What is it? Let me find out that Shaquan's dad is married."

My face pained, "Diamond you know I never believed in messing with a married man."

"Right, Right," Diamond guessed again, "Is he gay?"

"No! Sis he is not gay," I said while shaking my head.

Now Diamond is on the edge of her seat, "Well what is it?"

I responded, "Remember when Jamel asked me to come to New York after he left Atlanta."

"No, but go ahead."

"Anyway Jamel always complained how I never took Shaquan to Brooklyn to see him. I guess whenever Jamel got the itch to see his son he would call me and tell me he missed Shaquan.

One day he called me and disclosed his family was having a cook out and afterwards we were going to go to a club. He asked me to drive to New York. He explained to me his mom would babysit Shaquan while we go out. I was okay with it but I really didn't want to go because he told me he was working from 3p.m. to 11p.m. and I would have to go to the cook out without him. I decided to go and breezed in Brooklyn at 1:30p.m.

When I arrived Jamel was talking all of this rubbish about getting back together. I looked at him and told him I only came out here to party. I didn't even go to the cook out simply because I didn't want too."

Diamond intervened, "Sis why didn't you like him like that?"

"Because he was a compulsive liar, his lying turned me completely off."

"Sis a liar always got under your skin."

"Diamond, I can't stand them."

"You can't stand them because you put too much trust in people. Then when they lie on you or to you; you get emotionally disturbed."

"I really do, and then I will cut them off with no warning. Who wants to talk to a liar? Basically you are having a non – productive conversation, which is a waste of my time."

"Well, Twinkle if you stop trusting everyone then a liar would not bother you as much."

"I don't trust everyone; however I don't have time to entertain meaningless conversation. Any who, ever since Shaquan was born I tried to get child support but never was successful in doing so. I never understood it because Jamel stayed with a legit job and he would never give me anything for Shaquan."

"Word sis nothing!" Diamond said while being surprised.

"He wouldn't give me nothing. Basically after I had Shaquan I literally left him alone. The last time I messed with Jamel on that level was in Atlanta when I was going to Morris Brown and he was attending Clark University.

When I left Atlanta, I went to South Philly and stayed with Leroy for a while because I didn't feel like dealing with Mom and Dad."

Diamond chimed in, "I remember you and Leroy were high school sweethearts."

"Yes we were but we had broken up before I left to go to Atlanta because I found out Leroy was cheating on me with this girl named Penny. I don't know if you remember, but before I left to go to Atlanta I stayed with Leroy for four days. Remember his dad left him and his sister the house in South Philly?"

"That's right Twinkle they stayed having house parties."

"Yep and we stayed going to them.

On the last day right before I was about to leave. Leroy went to school, although he is six months older than me he was a grade behind me. While he was at school his house phone kept ringing it was nonstop.

Finally I picked up the phone, this lady in a nice manner asked could she speak to Leroy. I told her he was in school." Then she said, "Hello Brandi." That is Leroy sister name.

"I know Twinkle."

"Don't get sassy with me Diamond."

"Continue with the story, shoot I want to hear the secret because it's getting good."

"I told her I was not Brandi and that I was Leroy's girl Twinkle."

She replied Twinkle; "I am Leroy's lady Penny."

I responded, "Oh really, I've been with Leroy since we've been in the 10th grade."

Penny replied, "Little girl I'm thirty four years old, I've been with Leroy for eight months and I'm pregnant."

My heart dropped. I responded, "Do you know that Leroy is eighteen years old?"

She responded, "Yes, but Leroy is very mature for his age." Penny ended the phone call by saying, "May the best women win."

I responded, "Let the fun begin, and then hung up. I couldn't wait for Leroy to get home. When Leroy came home I told him off. Before he walked inside the house I started fighting him in my pajamas outside in the middle of the street."

Brandi came to the door because she was upstairs in her room she yelled, "Twinkle and Leroy get the hell in the house." I went into the house but Leroy didn't.

"Where did Leroy go?"

"I don't know sis. However, I laid on Brandi's bed and cried my little eyes out while telling her what happened."

Brandi tried to comfort me, "Twinkle that girl don't mean nothing to Leroy they are just phone buddies."

I responded, "Phone buddies with a baby on the way."

She said, "Twinkle that girl is not pregnant." Brandi continued to say, "When you go to college do you because Leroy is going to do him and neither of y'all are married."

"I took her advice and when I went to college 'I did me' and I told Leroy I had a boyfriend. Leroy would write me letters telling me he was sorry and hopefully when I come back to Jersey we could work things out. I asked Leroy about the baby he made clear Penny was lying. When I went to college I did me. Although Leroy was my high school boo deep down inside I knew we weren't going to last. I just couldn't trust him anymore.

Back to Jamel, when he went to work, I started to snoop and found paystubs under all of these papers that was made out to Greg John Steed."

Diamond said, "Oh No! This dude name is Greg?"

"Yes, Diamond! He told me his name was Jamel Matthew Steed. Diamond his mom never told me his real name nor did his family members. I remember one summer I went to a family gathering and I was smoking blunts with his cousins. One of the girl cousins asked me why I called him Jamel. I told her because that is his name.

I think she was about to tell me the truth but one of the other female cousins gave her a look like don't say nothing, but I caught the vibe. So quickly she said I've been calling him Sincere for so long I forgot his government name."

"That's right Twinkle that dude was a wannabe 5 percenter."

"Exactly," I rolled my eyes in disgust. "Anyway when Greg, (using his real name now) came home from work, I was elevated and ready to party. I knew when I got back to Jersey I was going right to the court house to get my child support checks."

"Twinkle I'm feeling your pain and what he did was real messed up but what is the secret?"

I got flip, "If you'll listen to the story you will find out. Fall back sis. Can I finish my story?"

"Yes, Twinkle and get out of your feelings."

"I'm not in my feelings but you are being real inconsiderate. Not only is this story personal it affects me and Shaquan greatly. Sis, please be patient it's hard for me to relive all of this."

"My bad," Diamond said, "I don't mean to come off insensitive but real talk I can careless about these dudes."

I huffed loudly. I continued to tell her the story. "When I returned to Jersey I gave the courts Greg's information and immediately I started to receive child support. Diamond remember when Shaquan's gear stepped up."

"Yeah, I remember."

"It was because I was getting those child support checks. For almost a year I was getting those checks. In the eleven month Greg requested a paternity test because he was aware that Leroy was my high school sweetheart. Greg was also aware I didn't I find out I was pregnant until I left Atlanta for summer break. Basically I was back home from college when I found out I was pregnant.

"How did Greg know Leroy was your high school sweetheart?" Diamond asked.

"I told him, like I told Leroy I was messing with Greg when I was in college. Diamond ain't nobody have time to be lying for the simple fact both of those dudes were doing them."

Diamond said, "Absolutely sis. The game goes both ways. But Twinkle I ain't telling nobody nothing. My motto is innocent until proven guilty. I'm not offering any information and if I get caught red handed I'm going to lie out of the lie."

"Diamond that is entirely too much thinking and remembering for me, my motto is, if I did it I'm going to let the individuals know. I gave them both the fair chance to leave or stay. They both decided to stay."

Diamond responded, "Yes sis, we just got it like that." She repeated, "We just got it like that."

"Eventually we went to the court house for the paternity test they swabbed me, Greg and Shaquan's mouth. When they swabbed Shaquan's mouth he was sleep."

The Judge asked, "Greg why did it take him so long for him to request a paternity test."

Greg stated, "That he was about to get married in a few months and his fiancé was with child."

I interjected, "Your Honor" the honest reason is because Greg lied to me about his name and I recently found out."

Greg with a major attitude burst out, "She was snooping."

The Judge being firm looked at me and asked, "Is this true?"

With confidence, I responded, "Yes-it-is."

"Good for you," the Judge responded, with a slight smirk. The female judge continued, "Mr. Steed the mother of your child should not have to snoop to find out your real name. The child is five years old and you should be ashamed of yourself."

"After the test was done, Greg took us out to eat. I think he was feeling a little guilty for lying to me about his name along with requesting a paternity test. While we were eating, I told him maybe when he finds out Shaquan is officially his he will become a better father. After we were done eating Greg took Shaquan to the park for a little while and then he left to go back to New York.

Two weeks later the results came in the mail. The results stated that Greg is the father.

However Jamel / Greg got in some trouble a few years back and he wanted me to be his alibi because he was facing a ten year prison term. So I lied to the police officers and convinced them he was with me, but actually he wasn't.

After he requested a paternity test, I decided to call NYPD and tell them his real name and that he was not with me. I put in plain English to NYPD I lied to them because I was afraid that Jamel would retaliate.

Shortly afterwards, Jamel was locked up for years."

"Twinkle, how do you know he got locked up?"

"Because his cousin Tyrone called me asking could I contribute to his bail? At the time Jamel was not aware that I snitched on him."

"Well how did he find out?"

"One day he called me from jail and out of anger I told him that I gave NYPD his real name and I also told NYPD he was not with me the day he committed the crime."

"Twinkle why did you tell him?"

"I was pissed; he kept calling me collect and asking me for money to put on his books. He had the audacity to ask me for money but couldn't tell me his real name. I expressed to him I will never give him anything and demanded for him to stop calling me."

"Wow!!!"

"Diamond he was so angry, he bid to me to watch my back. I bid to him to watch his ass. However, Greg reached out to me in the eighth year he was in jail via letter and mentioned he wanted to connect with Shaquan. Nonetheless, Shaquan was thirteen years old. Sis, I just didn't want to go down that road being he was known to be a liar."

"I feel you sis."

"He then rendered he gave his life to Christ. But don't they all when they get locked up. I wasn't trying to hear it, so I returned the letter and wrote I no longer live at this residence on the outside of the envelope.

Eventually when he got out he requested me to be a Facebook friend, he was inboxing me telling me how much he missed me. And was trying to talk slick. He still was up to no good. He was more worried about getting back with me than having a relationship with Shaquan.

After he got the memo I wasn't feeling him he deleted me. I guess he thought by deleting me I was going to feel some type of way. Diamond you know, I didn't care.

Diamond I never lied to Leroy or Greg and the reality is when you are 17, 18 and 19 years old nobody is faithful. But I was so angry that he asked for a paternity test."

"Twinkle nobody is faithful at any age."

"I disagree, everyone does not cheat. How I know, is because the entire time I was with Sly I never cheated on him because I really loved him."

"Damn sis! What the fudge cakes."

"Diamond that is new," we chuckled. I asked her was she trying to stop cussing.

"Yeah a little bit, we are getting older and the F word is so vulgar."

"Diamond I'm so glad you are growing up. You been cussing since you were five years old."

"I know, and you were always tattling."

"I sure was. Any who sis, I continued to take care of Shaquan and never told him the truth. When Shaquan would ask me where Jamel was because that is the name he knew him as. I would tell Shaquan I did not know and would change the subject. But deep down inside I knew Jamel wanted to get even with me."

"Dang Sis! I have a home-girl that is kind of in the same scenario. She told me she is never going to tell her kids their father is in jail and she is going to take that secret to her grave."

"After years went by I began to feel bad I called the police on him and told them the truth."

"Sis, Jamel… Greg whatever you want to call him put that on himself. Karma is real. If he couldn't do the time he shouldn't have did the crime. Real talk."

"Diamond, I decided I'm going to tell my son and just deal with the consequences. Me telling the truth thus far has never let me down."

"Twinkle a single mother struggle is real.

"But God is more real," I responded.

"Li'l sis, real talk, either this struggle can make you or break you. I chose for every good and bad situation to make me better than the day before. There were times in my life I wanted to run away from me and my issues but I realized that I cannot out run my problems. The only way to get rid of the problem is to confront them. If I don't, this problem is going to haunt me one-way or the other.

Diamond I made a lot of mistakes in my youth but now I know better so I must do better. As a Woman of God I can't continue to live a lie. I'm beginning to feel convicted because I know it's wrong. I've been lying out of fear and thinking about Shaquan's feelings.

However, the reality of it is, I've been really worried about my feelings due to my own selfish needs. But I have to tell Shaquan the truth and I am."

A look of shame took over Diamond countenance and she sadly said, "Twinkle we all have secrets."

"Would you like to tell me yours," I asked?

"No sis, I'll pass today."

"Diamond whatever happens; I have to trust God like never before. "

Right then Anisa walked in the house. She shouted, "Hey Mommy, hey Aunt D!" Anisa gave me a hug.

Diamond said, "Sis I'm going to the bakery to get some cupcakes so I will talk to you later."

"Alright," I responded.

That night I tossed and turned, I couldn't sleep because my mind was made up; I was going to tell Shaquan. I begin to pray. *Heavenly Father please forgive me for lying and not telling my son the truth about his father.*

Please give me the courage, wisdom and the strength to tell him the truth. I pray you will cover his emotions and mine as well. I ask you Father that Shaquan will not become bitter, unforgiving and hateful due to my lies and secrets.

Jesus I'm so sorry and although I'm saved I still have issues I must get delivered from however I refuse to continue to live a lie.

Shaquan is my son and I love him more than life itself. Help me Heavenly Father to tell him the whole truth. I rebuke the spirit of fear and procrastination in Jesus Name Amen.

The next morning Shaquan reminded me he didn't have work after school. Before he left for school, I asked him to come directly home right after school. Because I had to talk to him about something.

Shaquan being concerned asked, "If I was okay?"

In that moment I reassured my son that I was okay.

"Cool I will be here, but I wanted to hang with my boys after school."

"You still can because we are not going to be talking all day."

Shaquan smiled and said, "Yeah right mom. Remember today is hoop day Thursday."

On Thursdays he and his boys play basketball. He gave me a kiss on the cheek and left for school. Now I'm home alone and the house is quiet. So many thoughts were racing through my mind about Shaquan and Sly situation about his woman calling me.

I decided to drive to N.Y. to Jamel's mom's house to see if I could talk to him or find out where he was. I drove all the way to Bronx, N.Y. his mom's house was vacant.

I remembered where his cousin lived, thankfully his cousin lived fifteen minutes away. I arrived at Tyrone's house. I knocked on the door. A lady in her late 40's opened the door asked, "May I help you?"

"Hi my name is Twinkle does Tyrone live here?"

"Yes, what do you want with my man?"

"No disrespect, I have a son by his cousin Sincere and I'm looking for him."

"Tyrone is not here but Sincere is locked up."

"Again."

"Yes."

"Why?"

"He got caught stealing hypo allergenic pillows."

"Really pillows." I continued, "Is he smoking that stuff?"

"Girl no, he just didn't want to pay for them. Sincere told Tyrone he was tired of sneezing in the middle of the night."

I replied, "I bet you he is doing a lot of sneezing now... dummy." We both sniggered.

"Do you want Tyrone to give you Sincere's address to where he is locked up at?"

"No, I'm good, however please tell Tyrone I said hello."

"I will." She shut her door; I walked back to my car and drove back to New Jersey.

When I got home, I fixed myself a turkey and cheese sandwich and had some Lay's chips. I was chilling, just before I was done my door bell rung. *Now y'all know I don't like being disturbed while I'm eating.* So I took my last bite of my sandwich, ate my last chip and finished up my juice. I wasn't in a rush to answer the door because I didn't invite anyone over.

I looked through the peephole and guess who it was? It was the FedEx guy. I brushed my hair real quick and put a mint in my mouth before I answered the door. *You know you have to have that fresh breath.* He rang the doorbell again with aggression and kept ringing the doorbell.

I know this dude ain't ringing my doorbell like he has lost his mind. My smile instantly turned into a frown. I opened the door and yelled, "Why are you ringing my doorbell like there is a problem." He apologized.

"What do you want?" I asked in frustration?

Being polite he responded, "I want to personally thank you for directing me to the right address. Sometimes the way the numbers are numbered it can be a little confusing."

"Your welcome."

"What is your name?"

"Twinkle."

"Twinkle," he repeated while scratching his head.

"Yes!"

"Is that your real name?"

"My government is Lisa, but I'm known as Twinkle."

"What's your name?"

"Asurion."

Now rushing I said, "It was nice to meet you." All of a sudden I had to go to the bathroom. I thought to myself I know I'm not this nervous.

He asked could he come inside. I told him no as I walked outside. I'm looking at this dude like you are real bold to ask to come inside my house. Joker, I don't know you.

"Do you live around here?"

"No not really I live in Ewing, N.J."

"That's about a forty five minute ride from here."

"Yeah it's about that." Asurion acted if he was lost for words.

There was an awkward moment of silence. "Okay, Asurion it was nice meeting you but I was in the middle of doing something."

"Twinkle, I'm not trying to impose but are you in a relationship?"

"Why do you want to know?"

He replied, "I would like to take you out on a date if that's okay with you. I hope you are not feeling disrespected."

"No, I'm not but I was a minute ago when you asked to come inside of my home."

"I apologize for coming off a little strong."

As we were talking Pricy drove up. "Hey cuz," Pricy shouted when she got of her car. As she started to walk towards me she asked, "Why are you outside?"

"I can't be outside."

She ignored my flip response; "I came by to check on you. I bought you some juice and a few other things."

Asurion interjected, "I see that you are loved."

"Yes I am."

"Pricy this is Asurion. Asurion this is my first cousin Pricy." They both greeted one another.

"Pricy the door is unlocked you can go inside the house, I will be there in a few."

Pricy gave Asurion a questioning glance. She peeped something with him but I didn't care. He is fine with a good job; however I did notice he looked slightly different from the first time I saw him.

"Can I have your number Twinkle?"

"Are you married, divorced or with anyone because I'm not into game playing."

"No," he said while chuckling, he continued, "If I was divorced you wouldn't talk to me?"

"No I wouldn't."

"Why not," he asked being curious.

"I'm going to be my husband first and only wife and vice versa."

Asurion responded, "Okay" as if he was confused about my response.

"I'm just making sure you meet my standards before I give you my number." He grinned.

I started to tell him my number.

"Hold up," he interrupted. "Twinkle let me get my cell phone."

Impatiently, I looked at him. I repeated my number again.

"Thanks Twinkle I will call you later."

"Okay," I said while walking into my condo. As soon as I shut the door, Pricy announced, "Twinkle he is shifty."

"So are you."

"Twinkle, I'm serious please be mindful with him especially around the kids."

"First of all Pricy, I never had men around my children and I'm not going to start now."

"Twinkle something doesn't sit right with me."

"Whatever Pricy."

Pricy changing the subject, "Twinkle I came here to check on you and to make sure you were good."

"Thanks Pricy for coming through I appreciate it."

"I noticed your refrigerator is stocked," Pricy paused. "I see Sly has been around."

"Yes Pricy he has but not like that."

"Good!"

"Good for who Pricy?"

"Everyone Twinkle."

"Mmmm," I murmured.

"Are you still having shortness of breath?"

"I have my moments."

"Pricy I heard you be in Camden intimidating people to get saved and asking people do they know him?" Pricy started laughing.

"Twinkle I just don't want no one to go to hell. I know what God has delivered me from. I just want everyone to know Christ and experience his love because he is so faithful."

"Pricy I understand, but you can't scare people to Christ. The Bible says he/ she who wins souls to Christ is wise.

You have to love them to Christ and when you see them making mistakes you can't take it personal. You simply continue to pray for them. The bottom line, Pricy is we all have secrets and issues."

"Twinkle you have a secret? I sure do but not for long."

"I always admired your courage Twinkle."

"Pricy I've learned courage from being afraid and chose faith over fear. You know the scripture; God has not given us the spirit of fear but of power, love and a sound mind."

"Yeah I know it and I'm still working on it. Twinkle I've been wanting to tell you something for a while."

I responded, "What, you been dappling in that stuff again?"

"No! I mean, I still have crack dreams from time to time but I haven't given in."

"I'm proud of you Pricy because I know it's hard. Staying free is very hard. People really desire to see you fall and the majority of time it's your own family."

Pricy said, "Twinkle what gives you the desire to stay free?"

"Going back, isn't worth it. If people get mad at me and talk about me that's on them. I rather have people angry at me than to have an angry God. See when your life begins to transform for the better people start to hate on you.

People that operate in the Spirit of envy/ hate are actually operating in the spirit of murder. If they can't physically murder you, they will try to murder your name by lying and talking about you. But no weapon formed against me shall prosper. Please don't get it twisted Pricy I don't have it all together I'm a work in progress. Honestly, I'm still not totally free because I've been hiding something for a long time."

"Twinkle," she said as she took a deep breath. "I haven't been honest with you concerning me and Sly."

"What about you and Sly?"

"Twinkle the day you caught me mic- checking Sly it was not the first time."

"Pricy you told me it was."

With a look of shame, she continued. "The day you caught us I saw you peep in the room."

"Okay!" I responded.

"Twinkle, Sly and I were getting high in the same crack house for five years."

"I kind of figured you two crossed paths because you are the one who told me he was getting high."

"Twinkle" she paused. "Sly and I was also having sexual relations. That day when you saw him rape me he really didn't because I was down with it, and been down with it for five years."

"What were you trying to do?" being whimsical I replied. "Keep it in the family."

"Twinkle I'm sorry, I'm so sorry. I wasn't in my right mind and neither was Sly. God has delivered me and I want to be totally free. Eventually you would have found out and I wanted to be the one to tell you."

"Damn Pricy! This is messed up," now yelling, "You know how much I loved him."

Pricy screaming, "Twinkle please forgive me."

"Forgive you Pricy foreal." Now screaming back, "That's what you came up with. You are out of your rabbit cracked out mind. You were sleeping with Sly for five years, was it some sick game you and him were playing?

I'm sure it was mad smokers in the crack house you could of chose from, but you chose Sly? I hate you and I'm tired of forgiving you. So when Sly was calling you to check up on Anisa y'all were having phone sex and laughing behind my back. While y'all were smashin' did you ask him who was better?

This explains why Sly never liked you because he knew you were shady. Sly knew you never loved me because he told me you didn't. You always hated on me and wanted to be me. So you decided to have sex with my man for five years to prove what Pricy. Since the cat has your tongue, I will answer. To prove you are a nasty stank hoe. Are y'all still smashin' because obviously you caught feelings?"

"I never meant to hurt you Twinkle," she said while crying."

"One day I was in the crack house and I was waiting to get high with someone. I saw Sly walk in but I acted like I didn't see him. Sly saw me, he had crack and wanted to smoke."

He asked me, "What's up!"

"I told him you."

He said, "Lets' go in the bathroom so we didn't have to share with anyone else. There was a small radio in the bathroom, he told me to dance for him. While he was smoking I was stripping eventually Sly unzipped his pants, I gave him a lap dance and one thing led to another."

"Pricy what if I punch you in your face right now? What would you do?" Pricy was crying and gasping for air as she repeatedly stated she was sorry.

"Don't gasp now Pricy!"

She screamed, "Twinkle I hated you."

"You hated me Pricy," now yelling back. "I never did anything to you but love you and stick up for your simple behind."

"Every time Sly and I would smash, he would tell me to turnaround because he didn't want to look at my face. I wanted him to love me the way he loved you. Now Pricy hysterically yelling Twinkle I always wanted to be you."

"Pricy all of that screaming doesn't move me in matter of fact get the hell out of my house and scream some more outside."

Pricy walked real fast out the house while side eyeing me. I guess she thought I was going to punch her in her throat. All of the anger I felt from years ago started to manifest.

I wanted to smoke a blunt so bad. I haven't smoked in ten years I don't even know who's selling it. I started screaming in my house, I wanted to drive to Philly and kick Sly's door down again.

All of these wrong emotions and wrong thoughts started to enter my mind. I wanted to get a skunk, kill it and put it in front of Sly's door. I hated Sly and I hated Pricy. I started pacing back and forth in my Condo. I started talking to myself.

My phone rung and broke me out of my trance. "What," I answered while being in an unhealthy mental state.

"Sister," she said humorously, "Where is the hostility coming from?"

I started to explain to Diamond what happened.

"Lisa! Lisa! Calm down." Now shouting calm down.

"Diamond Yo! Family always trying to break me, they try to break my spirit; they want me bitter, and crazy just like them."

"Sis! Tap into your euphoric emotion and coping skills."

"Sis this is not the time for your stupid jokes."

Diamond being serious. "Lisa you are mentally unstable right now and I'm not joking. Real talk sis count to ten, inhale and exhale. You just got out of the hospital and you need to chill. Pricy was wrong but she is family and family still comes first."

"Diamond you're right family does come first but I don't have to put up with family betrayal. This drama right here is not worth it."

"Twinkle you love Pricy."

"Diamond I don't want to hear that shit."

"Well you're going to hear it and get your mind right. Sly is shady he done smashed mad chicks, put his hands on you, lied to you and don't do shit for Anisa and you forgave him over and beyond. But you are trippin' about our cousin who was brave and honest enough to tell you the truth. This was hurting Pricy more than you think and the guilt was eating at her."

"Diamond you acting like you knew about this."

"Twinkle I did."

"Diamond you knew and didn't tell me. Why didn't you tell me?"

"Because I knew you were going to act like this." Diamond trying to lighten the situation. "Remember my ex smashed my home girl?"

Yelling, "Diamond it wasn't your cousin."

"Twinkle it doesn't matter that is how dude's operate."

"Diamond do we still have the same last name? The last time I checked both of our last names…" now screaming, "Is Valentine. Team V! But it appears to me you are on Team P standing for Pricy/ Punk! And Team S for Sly /Shady! That's how you're getting down sis? You are just as Shady as Team S and P."

Diamond replied, "That's umbrella shade the clouds are moving in and it's getting dark outside shade."

"Oh! You're really trying to reverse this back on me. Yo! Diamond I have no rap!" I banged on her.

Diamond called right back and said, "Sis pray for those who despitefully use you. I love you and I always will be on Team V we share the same DNA and always will. Word is Bond!"

I broke and started crying while Diamond was on the phone.

"Twinkle I know you are hurt but you have to forgive and then let it go. Nobody's perfect and in order to move on you have to forgive Sly and Pricy, not for them but for you. God has great things in store for you and unfortunately but fortunately this is part of the process.

God orders the steps of a good woman. Twinkle real talk you're going have to eat it. You are not with Sly and Pricy is family. Counted all joy you don't mess with Sly anymore."

"Thanks Diamond! I'm going to talk to you later. I have to get my thoughts together."

Before we hung up, Diamond said, "Twinkle tap into your euphoric emotion."

"Perplexed," I said "Diamond how am I going to do that?"

She responded, "Do what you do best and pray."

"Okay! Diamond I'll talk to you later. Wait! Diamond why did you call me?"

Diamond responded, "I had to tell you something but I will tell you later. Right now, Twinkle your emotions are too fragile."

"Really Diamond fragile? Okay and good-bye."

I prayed and asked God to help my unstable emotions. I started to feel a little better. I drank some of the juice Pricy brought over; I looked at my glass and started to get angry again. So I threw the glass in the sink and got me a bottled of water. Yea! I was buggin'. I sat on the couch and woosah, and then started asking myself why was I so angry?

Truth be told I already knew Pricy had insecure issues, so did Sly. And real talk so did I. Am I really better? No I am not. I have a secret I still didn't tell my son. This thing called life is some ish.

I drifted off to sleep on my couch and was awakened by Shaquan as he walked into the house.

"What's up Mom?"

"What's up," sounding groggily while just waking up? "What time is it, I asked?"

"It's 3:30p.m. I dosed off and was in my bag."

"Where is Anisa?"

"Anisa texted me and asked could she go over Trinity's house after school because they have a project due soon."

"Oh!" Shaquan responded.

It was a brief moment of silence. Sounding a little impatient Shaquan said, "Mom what do you need to talk to me about?"

"Son, what I'm about to tell you is not easy for me. You will be graduating from High School and then going to the Army.

I'm very proud of you."

Shaquan responded, "Okay Mom I already know what you're going to tell me."

"You do," I responded while being surprised.

"Yea!"

"Well what is it?" I asked.

"Mom you are back messing with Sly again." He continued, "I'm not even mad because you need a man around while I'm gone."

"Son that's what you came up with all by yourself?" I said while being cynical."

"I know Sly still loves you and I know you still love him."

"How do you know Sly still loves me?"

"Mom I know these things."

"Ok Shaquan! Sly is a cheater and that is not love. And for your information no I don't mess with Sly and I'm not going too."

"Then what is it?"

Straightforwardly I said, "Son, Jamel is not your father's real name. His name is Greg and he was in prison for ten years."

"What Mom?"

"Jamel lied to me about his name and when you were five years old, I found out that his real name was Greg.

He asked for a paternity test almost a year after I found out his real name. I got so angry I snitched on him. He had got in some trouble when we were kicking it. As a result of me snitching he did ten years in prison. I was too fearful to tell you the truth but now since I'm trying to live an honest and a better life I want all of my skeletons out of my closet."

"Mom you got my Dad locked up?"

"Yes and no."

"What did he get locked up for?"

"I believe armed robbery, but I'm not sure."

"Mom, why are you telling me this now," his nose flared?

"Because you are about to transition to another phase of life and I thought you would be able to handle the truth."

"Damn Mom! You've known this since I was five and you are just telling me now."

"Shaquan, I'm sorry, your Mom was a coward. I wish I was brave enough to tell you sooner but I wasn't."

"Do you know where he is?"

"Yes, he is back in jail."

"For what?"

I was too embarrassed to tell Shaquan he was in jail for stealing freakin' hypo allergenic pillows.

"I'm not sure."

"Mom this is messed up. All that praising God is a front. You always tell me and Anisa to keep it real and be honest, and you of all people weren't being honest. Isn't that called being a hypocrite?"

"Call me what you want, I'm still your Mom. I am human, I made a mistake and I'm sorry I didn't tell you immediately after I found out."

"No! Mom, you didn't make a mistake nor did you lie you just told me a story."

"Shaquan you are really getting loose with your mouth. I'm letting you slide because I understand you are angry. But please don't take my kindness for my weakness."

"Whatever," he said as he stormed out of the house.

When he left I started to cry. This was the first time we had a real disagreement. I knew he was angry and he had all the right to be. The same grace Pricy wanted me to show her. Is the same grace I wanted Shaquan to show me. How hypocritical is that?

I wanted to go to the liquor store and purchase some Henny but I knew that Anisa would be home soon. Anisa never saw me drink anything but water and juice. I don't know how she would respond if she saw me drinking. I don't need for her to be hurt.

Shaquan being hurt is already too much for me. Me knowing he is hurt because of my past mistakes hurts me even the more. My son doesn't deserve this, he is a good kid. I never had any real problems from him. I had typical teenage issues but nothing ever serious.

I have been very blessed. God I need your help. I need you to heal Shaquan's broken heart and please cover him. I felt so bad; Shaquan never came home that evening. I called his cell phone a few hours later just to see how he was doing.

When he answered the phone he voiced he wasn't coming home and was staying over his girlfriend's house. I articulated I loved him he responded, "Okay Mom" then hung up the phone.

Chapter 4
Scheming

Today is payday Friday, after Anisa left for school. I decided to get a sew-in, a full body wax and massage. Maybe if I get myself together I will feel better. Being off of work was beginning to become depressing along with the other issues I was dealing with.

I contacted my hairdresser early; I have the best hair stylist because she comes to my house. She came at 10:00 a.m. and was done my hair by 12:30p.m. Afterwards, I went to the spa, got my wax, massage, pedicure and manicure. After I was done I felt like a million bucks.

While I was getting my pedicure Asurion called me.

"How are you doing Lady?"

"Very well thank you," I replied.

"Twinkle do you have plans for this Saturday."

"I'm not sure why?"

"I want to take you out if that's okay with you."

"What time?"

"Around 1:30p.m, I was thinking of taking you to Penn's Landing so we could go on the boat ride. Afterwards to the Charter House to get something to eat."

"That sounds nice, let me check on some thing's and call you back this evening."

When I hung up the phone I was hype, I was asked to go on a date. It's been years. Thank God I decided to get my hair and nails done.

I started to think about who was going to watch Anisa?

Shaquan has not been here and my parents most likely will be busy. Diamond is funny acting because she likes to party. I can't leave her home alone because she is only ten. I decided to ask Sly, besides he is her father.

I went and bought me a cute sundress and some sharp sandals. On my way home, I saw Anisa walking so I picked her up.

"Hey Mommy, you look beautiful."

"Thanks Honeybun, I had to get myself together."

After we got settled in the house, I told Anisa I had something to tell her.

"What is it Mommy?"

"Mommy is going on a date tomorrow with a man I met not too long ago."

"Where did you meet him at?"

I told her it was the FedEx guy. She responded, "Good Mommy, you deserve to enjoy yourself."

"Thanks Honeybun. I'm going to call your dad and ask him if he can pick you up and take you to his crib.

After my date is over I'll pick you up. Most likely I shouldn't be out past 10p.m."

Anisa changing the subject asked, "Where is my brother?"

"He's been over his girlfriend's house, he and I got into a disagreement."

"What about?"

"I'll tell you one day, just not today but he will be okay."

"Just like you say Mommy, this too shall pass."

"It sure will."

"When are you going to call Daddy?"

"Right now."

I dialed his number and of course he didn't pick up. I didn't bother to leave a message. I went on with my day; I fixed dinner while Anisa did her homework.

Around 9:30p.m. Sly called me. When I answered, I noticed his speech was slurred. "VP you called me?"

"Sly are you saucy?"

"Nah, but I'm feeling right."

"Oh, You in your zone."

"You trying to be funny VP?"

"Sly first of all, I am not your vanilla pound cake, when I was, you didn't appreciate it."

"I miss you VP."

"I know you miss me, the reason why we are not together is because you miss everybody. You want a quick fix and quick fixes are for your nominees. What you don't realize is there is only one Grammy award winner which is me."

"Okay Twinkle you are messin' with my high."

"Good Sly, Did I talk you down?"

"Yea, What's up?"

"I need you to do me a favor. Saturday, Shaquan and I have to meet with his Sergeant at 10:45a.m. and I don't want to leave Anisa home by herself. Can you pick her up at 10:00 a.m.? When the appointment is over I will come and get her."

"Shaquan is really going into the military," Sly responded.

"Yeah, he is."

"I'm so proud of that dude; I remember when I was changing his diapers," Sly reminiscing.

"Are you going to watch Anisa at your house?"

"Yeah."

"Thank you Sly."

"Twinkle why are you being so nice."

"Because it is nice to be nice, you should try it sometime."

"Alright Twinkle."

"See you Saturday at 10:00a.m."

Now I know y'all are saying why did she lie to Sly. And I should have told him the truth. We all know if we tell our baby fathers we are going on a date, they are not going to show. They barely show up when everything is good.

Look I'm ready to go out and have adult conversation with a fine man, shoot I've been through a lot and I need some rest and relaxation.

Don't forget, we all know the real reason why Sly called me drunk. He thought I was going to cuss him out because I found out about his girl and their child. Mind you he still doesn't know that I know about him and Pricy. I ain't even trippin' no more.

I texted Asurion and told him Saturday at 1:30p.m. is good. Asurion texted me, "see you then."

Before I went to bed I texted Shaquan, "love you."

He texted back, "lv u 2."

I texted him, "where are u?"

He texted back, "at grandma's."

I'm not surprised that my parents didn't tell me about Shaquan staying at their house. Normally, I would of called them but Shaquan is about to graduate from high school in a month. The most important factor is he's safe.

I texted Shaquan, "good night."

Before I drifted off to sleep, I asked God for forgiveness for lying, I also asked him to forgive me for all of my mistakes and bad choices that are affecting my son.

You know when you are young sometimes you don't think about how your decisions will affect your children in a negative way. Sometimes your fear does more harm to your child than good.

The last thing I want to do is to hurt my children. I have to believe God will work this out for my good some crazy way. When things appear to be falling apart sometimes things are actually falling in place. You can't change the past but you can have a better future.

Chapter 5

What You Do In the Dark Will Come To The Light

Today is Saturday, I'm amped. When I woke up I fixed Anisa and I breakfast and started my Saturday chores. Anisa lounged around waiting for her dad to come and get her. Around 12:00 p.m. I called Sly, he didn't answer. I waited for fifteen minutes then called him again. Still no answer, so I decided to leave him a message asking him if he was still going to watch Anisa.

I broke down and called Diamond. I made known to her I'm going on a date with the FedEx dude and asked could she watch Anisa to at least 7p.m. Worse come to worse me and dude will go to Penn's Landing and then start heading back to Jersey around 5p.m.

Diamond agreed to watch Anisa. She stated she won't be home until 1:00 p.m. She went to work for some overtime. Before I could respond, Diamond said sis, "Better yet, I will pick Anisa up after I get off of work."

"Thanks sis for looking out."

"Sis no problem, you only live once. Plus it doesn't make any sense for you to drive Anisa to my crib, when I'm getting off in about an hour."

"Thanks Again! I'll see you in a few."

I explained to Anisa; Aunt Diamond is going to watch her because I wasn't sure if her dad was coming. She was cool with it.

"Mom, I love hanging with Aunt Diamond because she orders me whatever I want and I can always convince her to take me to the mall. I love Aunt Diamond's swag."

"So do I, Aunt Diamond was always sharp even when we were kids."

"Mommy I also love the way she drives. She drives like the actors in the movie *Fast and Furious.*"

We started laughing. But quickly told her, Aunt Diamond better adhere to the speed limit when she has my Honeybun in the car.

"Oh! Mommy loosen up."

"Honeybun there is a reason why we have seat belts and speed limits."

"I know; I know seat belts save lives.

I always tell Aunt Diamond what you say. Aunt Diamond always says 'her defensive driving skills are on point.'"

"Anisa tell Aunt Diamond she can drive lawless when you are not in the car with her. Honeybun, Aunt Diamond will be here before you know it. Let me start getting ready."

"Okay Mommy!"

I turned on the radio and started to get dressed. Shortly afterwards Diamond knocked on the door. I opened the door. As she walked in she said, "What's up sis."

"Hey!"

"What time is Oh boy coming?"

"He should be here at 1:30p.m."

"Okay well I'm going to take Anisa now."

"Good look sis."

When Diamond opened the door Sly was about to ring the doorbell, this dude had the balls to waltz right on in my house like he was on time.

I spazzed out, "Sly it's too late you were supposed to be here at 10:00a.m. It's 1:20p.m. How are you just going to come darn near three hours later? I told you, Shaquan and I had a meeting with his Sergeant at 10:45a.m."

Right before Sly was about to respond, Shaquan walks into the house.

"What's up Shaquan," Sly said.

"What's good Sly?"

Sly apologizes to Shaquan. "I'm sorry man for not coming sooner so you and your mom could go see your Sergeant."

"What are you talking about?" Shaquan asked Sly.

"I interjected; okay Sly you can leave now."

"Twinkle what's going on?"

"None of your business Sly."

Sly sounding pitiful, "I brought some paint over and was going to paint Anisa's room instead of taking her to Philly."

"Sly how are you just going to intrude like that, just leave Sly."

Shaquan chimes in, "Mom what's going on?"

"It's a long story son."

Shaquan responded, "I'm not surprised."

I gave him the evil eye like boy don't press your luck.

Diamond trying to break the monotony jokingly said, "I'm glad to see everyone. I wish I would have known everyone was going to show up because I would have brought a bottle."

Now I'm trying to get everyone out of the house before dude rings the doorbell. Sly peeped I was trying to rush him out.

"Twinkle, you never been good at being sneaky."

"Okay Sly, so just leave then."

The doorbell rings. I was hesitant to open the door because I knew it was Asurion.

With aggression Sly demanded, "Open the door Twinkle."

"Sly, how about you answer the door since you are leaving. You weren't supposed to be here anyway you Nut."

I opened the door and Asurion was holding a bouquet of flowers looking fine and smelling good. I felt like time stopped for a few seconds.

"Hi Asurion, come in," I said with a flirty smile. While he was given me the bouquet of flowers Sly said, "who dis' Twinkle?"

"Again none of your business."

Asurion being concerned asked me, "If he came at a bad time."

"We are just in a middle of a family feud. Could you please wait outside? I'll be there in a few minutes."

Asurion responded, "No problem."

"Thank you."

"Who's that Mom?" asked Shaquan?

"That's my friend Asurion and we are going on a date."

"I thought you and Shaquan was going to talk to his Sergeant," Sly said while trying to instigate the situation.

"Now you know Sly you are not the only one who knows how to lie. How does it feel? How does your lying medicine taste? You can't swallow it, can you?"

"He's shifty Twinkle."

"So are you, it takes one to know one."

Diamond co- signed, "Sis he is fine, but something is not right with him."

"Again Diamond do we have the same last name? Whose side are you on? I responded, whatever."

"Mommy something is fishy about him."

I bent down on one knee and said, "Honeybun, I know you want me and your dad to be together but our relationship is over."

"That's what your mouth is saying," Sly blurted.

I ignored him. I gave Anisa a kiss on the cheek. "Okay, I'm leaving now and you all can figure out who is watching Anisa since all of y'all are here." Being a smart-alecky I continued, "Maybe all of y'all can watch her, talk crap about me and tell each other how shifty my new dude is."

I started to walk towards the door.

"Wait!" Diamond shouted, "Sis wait. We need to be on one accord before you just jet out of here."

"Oh boy is waiting for me," I yelled back.

"Sis, I don't care about him. He can wait all day. Really Twinkle, who is he?"

"Yea, Diamond," Sly responded.

Diamond looked at Sly and replied, "This is not the time. Real talk if you weren't Anisa's dad your ass would be outside, right along with him too. Stay in your lane Sly. Stay in your lane. This convo is between me and my sister."

Shaquan intervening, "Mom I came over because I wanted to talk to you."

"Shaquan I'm going out, we will talk later."

"I'm going to stay here and watch Anisa," Sly insisted. "I brought paint over and I'm going to paint her room."

"Sly, I don't know what time I'm coming back and I don't want you blowing up my phone."

"Ain't nobody thinking about you Twinkle."

"Good on that note I'm out. Diamond, thank you for coming, I apologize for inconveniencing you. We will talk later. Shaquan and Anisa I love y'all, see you later tonight."

"Mommy what time will you be home?"

"I'm not sure baby but I will call you shortly."

Chapter 6
Let the Fun Begin

I walked out of the door. Asurion had a black Infinity truck and it was sharp. He opened the passenger door and I stepped in with poise. He closed the door like a gentleman.

"You look stunning," he said as he started driving off.

"Thank you!"

When he was driving I noticed a medium size spider tattoo on his right hand, which I didn't noticed before.

"I didn't know you had a son."

"I do, he is seventeen years-old and my daughter is ten years old. Do you have any children?"

"No."

"That's surprising. How old are you?"

Asurion replied, "Forty-three."

I kept looking at the spider tattoo. Asurion noticed and asked me was I okay?

"When did you get the tattoo?"

"I been had it?"

"No you didn't, I would have noticed it the day you ask me to sign off on the package."

"Okay Twinkle, okay, you caught me he started to grin. I just got it the other day. Do you like it, he asked as he showed it off?"

"No, I don't like spiders."

"I do and when I was younger the 'Itsy Bitsy Spider' was my favorite nursery rhyme."

This dude broke out and started singing the lullaby lyrics to the Itsy Bitsy Spider, then started doing the hand gestures that mimic the words of the song sounding and looking real cra, cra. I looked at him with the blank expression.

Interrupting him, I said, "You need to keep your hands on the wheel. Where are we going?"

"Oh my bad Twinkle I was reliving my childhood moment," he said with a smirk. "To answer your question we are going to Penn's Landing? Our boat ride is scheduled for 3:00 o'clock."

"So was that your child's father?"

"Yes, He was supposed to pick up my daughter earlier but he came when he felt like it."

"How long have you been working for FedEx?"

"For four years."

"Where are you from?"

"Originally North Jersey, Newark."

"Why did you move to Ewing?"

I noticed Asurion beginning to get agitated like I was asking him too many questions. Being short he replied, "I needed a change."

"Where are you from?"

"I'm from Willingboro, NJ."

"You're from the suburbs, y'all are fresh," he said with a devious smile. It appeared he went somewhere in his mind that I didn't want to go. I started to feel uncomfortable.

I responded, "Don't let the freshness fool you boo."

"You're a feisty one too."

"If you say so."

"I like feisty," he said with a smirk.

I gave him the side eye. I thought; this dude is truly a weirdo.

"Can you turn on the radio?"

I needed to hear something that was familiar, this dude is clearly bonkers.

"Sure Twinkle."

DMX – "What They Really Want" ft. Sisqo was on. I started snapping my fingers and boppin' my head. I was jamming.

Asurion interrupting me. "Twinkle I see you like to dance."

"Dude you are killin' my vibe, can I just listen to my song and be in my zone."

"Calm down Twinkle, I was just trying to make conversation."

"Okay lets converse after my song goes off."

We finally arrived. Asurion parks and opens the door for me. He held my hand as he helped me out of the truck. We boarded, "The Patriot for Philadelphia Ultimate Harbor Cruise." The Patriot is a reproduction of the 1920's commuter yacht. This yacht setting was very intimate. It felt so good to just get away from everybody and everything.

This harbor cruise departed from the Independence Seaport Museum and provided an hour cruise of the Delaware River. This cruise was lightly narrated. During the cruise I saw the historic vessels of Penn's Landing, the tall ship Gazela, the Ben Franklin Bridge and Philadelphia's Race Street Pier.

We saw Camden Waterfront including the Battleship, and the Adventure Aquarium and Campbell's Field. This cruise went all the way down to the Delaware River. The Patriot had a very nice bar with beer, wine and mixed drinks. I was enjoying the scenery.

Asurion asked, "Do you want something to drink?"

I responded, "Yes."

Mind you the last time I drunk anything was nine years ago. I figured one drink wasn't going to hurt anything. I rationalized, all of the drama I am going through, I deserve a drink. After all, I needed something to take this edge off. I told him I wanted a Pineapple Cîroc. I thought that was better than getting Henny.

Asurion ordered a Sky Blue. We started drinking and I started to feel better. Once the courage juice started to settle in, he started to tell me how beautiful I was and how he never saw someone so gorgeous.

I'm looking at this dude, like your flattering tactics are so corny. I wanted to say so bad, the only reason why I'm beautiful is because you want some. But instead I said thank you.

Asurion started to open up telling me he really didn't like his job, because he and his boss are not getting along.

I asked him, "Why?"

"My boss gives me the runs that are out of the way."

"How far do you travel?"

"Sometimes I travel as far as New York."

I didn't say anything, but remember I saw his work van in my complex and he told me he lives in Ewing, NJ. Maybe he has a girlfriend around where I live?

Interrupting my thoughts, "Twinkle do you enjoy your job?"

"Yes," before I could tell him the reason why, his cell phone rang. As he picked up he started to walk away. I started to make conversation with the other people that were on the yacht.

When he came back ten minutes later, I asked him "Was he alright?"

"Yes," he said as he walked to the bar and ordered Vodka.

He started drinking and his whole vibe changed and his energy was off. It was like whoever called him gave him some bad news, he was real quiet. *I kept saying to myself I can't wait until this boat ride is over.* Finally, when the boat ride was over he asked me was I hungry?

"Yes, I am."

As he was driving to the restaurant, he told me one time he was driving drunk. When the police stopped him; he got locked up. He continued, "At the precinct they gave me a Breathalyzer test and when they printed the report. The report indicated I was over the alcohol limit so I grabbed the paper and ate the report." Then he started to laugh.

I gave him a paralyzing stare and asked, "Did they print the report again?"

He responded, "You don't even want to know."

I wanted to tell him a few years ago I got bit by a pit bull and two days later I went to the owner's house, jumped the fence and threw one towel over the pit's face. Threw another towel on his body and bit the pit back. But he wasn't ready, so I just let him imagine his corny story was funny.

We got seated in the restaurant; the waitress asked did I want something to drink? I told her Henny. This dude ordered Rum. Wasn't he just drinking Vodka? You know how it is when you start mixing brown and clear liquor. The waitress came back with my drink and I drunk my Henny in 2.5. Just when I was done my drink Anisa called me. "Mommy can you come home now?"

"Is everything okay?"

"No! Daddy and Aunt Diamond are arguing because she never left." She continued, "Aunt Diamond said 'she wanted to watch me and Daddy told her he was going to watch me.'

I just want the whole world to know my sister is going in Sly's mouth hard and she has my full support. Sly caused all of this confusion because he came late. Now he's trying to regulate and act like father of the year. Not on my watch.

"Anisa let me speak to Aunt Diamond?"

Diamond shouted, "Sis I'm about to break this dude's face."

I started cracking up. Diamond yelled, "I'm glad you think this is funny."

"Diamond chill for a second, and hear me out. Take Anisa with you." I paused, "Diamond hold on real quick."

The waitress came to our table asking us were we ready to order. I answered her no. Please give me a few more minutes. I caught Asurion looking at the waitress behind when she walked away. He looked at her like he wanted to eat her.

"Diamond, take Anisa with you. I'm on my way. I will deal with Sly later."

I hear Sly yelling in the background, "I don't care, Anisa is my daughter."

"Your commentary is not necessary, don't nobody care that you're my niece dad. I'm her Aunt and been here since day one. You give my niece $358.00 every year. You are so stupid you don't even realize there is 365 days in a year."

Diamond now screaming louder. "What! You give her a dollar a day Sly? Oh my bad you subtract a dollar from the seven National holidays. That's what you do, because you're a National dead beat."

I interjected, "Sis did you just say the seven national holidays?"

"Yes I did."

Diamond what are the seven national holidays.

"Really sis?"

"I'm so serious Diamond."

"New Years' Day, Memorial Day, Independence Day, which Sly celebrates because the only person he cares about is himself. Labor Day which you should celebrate Twinkle because you do all of the labor. Thanksgiving, Christmas - thank God for Jesus and Martin Luther King Day – "I have a dream" the only one dreaming is my niece wishing for a better dad."

I told y'all my sis was going in Sly's mouth. I will never look at the seven National Holidays the same again.

"Diamond give the phone to Sly and take Anisa and leave."

"Alright sis!"

Sly hollering, "Twinkle, I'm here trying to paint Anisa's room and your sister is trippin'."

"Okay! I told her to take Anisa. As a matter of fact I'm on my way home. So you can leave Sly and put Anisa's phone on the table."

Sly banged on me. I asked Asurion could he take me home.

"Is everything okay Twinkle?"

"Yes, I just need to handle something."

I began to feel woozy. I just wanted to go home and go to sleep. While Asurion was driving me back he stated he had a nice time with me. I was speechless and turned up a little because I was drinking on an empty stomach.

When we arrived at my place he asked me did I want him to walk me to my door.

"No, I'm good. Thank you!"

He opened the passenger door and I stumbled out. I didn't want him to help me because I didn't want him to try to force his way into my house.

I tripped going up my stairs; I finally made it to the front door. I unlocked my door, turned around and waved bye. He smiled, waved back then sped off.

Chapter 7

I Can't with This Dude

When I opened the door Sly was sitting on my couch watching TV. Instantly I rolled my eyes and sighed.

"What are you doing here Sly?"

Sly ignored my question and said, "You're drunk Twinkle."

I started dancing a little and responded, "Yep and there's nothing you can do about it. What you can do is take your black ass home. Hey!!!"

I flopped down on the sofa opposite of where Sly was sitting.

"How was your date Twinkle?"

"Great! If I knew you were still here I would of drunk some more."

"Were you drinking Henny?"

"I sure was big daddy."

"I remember how Henny used to make you feel."

Being flirtatious, "You do."

Sly walked over to me and started kissing me; I felt his hand going up my sundress. I wanted him; it's been years since I got any. I'm tipsy and ready. Hell, why not?

We continued kissing and then Sly removed my panties. In my head I'm saying it's about to go down. He started touching my sweet pink and said, "Yea it's talking."

I responded, "Yea it's talking and it's trying to have a conversation with you."

Sly whispered in my ear, "You know what to do?"

I came out of my zone and asked, "What do you want me to do?"

"Turnaround."

"Oh! I whispered back that's how you want it?"

"Yeah," he responded.

"Sly let's go into the bedroom."

We walked in the bedroom; I got on the bed and assumed the position. I started shaking my behind like it was a saltshaker.

Sly started slapping my behind; he said, "Yea I knew you would eventually give in. I knew you couldn't stay away for long."

Sly unzipped his pants and pulled out a condom. *Hold up, why does he have a condom? Furthermore you only use condoms with people you don't trust.*

Just before he entered me I turned around and back slapped him, so hard in the face he wasn't hard no more.

Station identification break, did y'all think Twinkle was going out like that? If you did, you must not know about me.

He might have got some, if he didn't tell me to turnaround. Remember, Pricy told me that's how he used to sex her.

God always knows how to show up and snap you back into reality.

Sly is yelling as he is zippering his pants, "What the F&$# is wrong with you?"

I jumped off the bed, and yelled in Sly's face. "Punk did you really think I was going to allow you to assassinate my character? You've been smashing Pricy on and off for years. Oh! What you didn't think I knew."

Sly responded, "I should"... before he finished I responded, "Take your ass home."

He mushed my face.

I spit in his face and said, "What! I'm ready it's been years, my weight and energy is up."

"Twinkle, you are going to get yours," he shouted as he walked out of the room.

I started laughing, and singing, "Payback is a mutha. Who's laughing now?" I continued, "Nananaaaaaaa boo boo you can't smash me." He stormed out of the house.

I walked back into my room and popped in a flick did my one, two and as soon as I climaxed. I immediately ran into the bathroom and started vomiting.

While I was hovered over the toilet I started crying and asking God for forgiveness, I felt so convicted on so many levels.

When you open the door to the devil he's going to come in every door, I had no business drinking. Although I didn't know Sly was still at my house the devil did and he was trying to set me up.

After I finished vomiting, I kneeled down on my bedroom floor and told God I was so sorry. I had thrown all of my flicks away but this particular one. I was so angry at myself, I saw myself going backwards. I was doing so well. I thought I was delivered?

Clearly I still had something's in me I didn't know was still there. I prayed and cried so much I cried myself to sleep.

Chapter 8
Hungry

Hours later I was awakened by my cell phone.

"Hello," I answered.

"Yo! Sis," It was Diamond. She asked was I good?

"I'm hungry," I answered.

"Well eat Twinkle."

"Diamond I don't feel good, I drunk Cîroc and Henny on empty stomach, I began to cry."

"Sis get your mind right, you are not going to hell because you had two baby drinks."

I started to snicker. "Diamond it's been darn near a decade since I drunk anything? Then I almost slipped up."

Diamond curiously repeated, "Slipped up? What you was about to puff on that Exotic? My older sis is an undercover bad girl."

"This is not funny and I wasn't about to puff on no exotic. I was about to smash Sly."

"Sis, really Sly, I might of got excited if you said the other dude but Sly sis. Unbelievable!"

"I'm so mad at myself. I acted like I was going to smash him and assumed the positon."

Diamond replied, "What! Oh gosh, the car is about to crash, air bags please save me. Back up, now elevating her voice repeated 'assumed the position'?"

"Yes, right before he entered me I turned around and back slapped him in his face."

"No!!! Twinkle!!!"

"Yes, Sly tried to play me, afterwards I spit in his face."

"Twinkle I want you to hear me and hear me good. We don't want you drinking anymore."

"Who is 'we' Diamond?"

Diamond raising her voice, "The world! Your mood is too rude and you tap into a whole other evil."

"I guess the saying is true Diamond. If you dance with the devil he will kiss you right in the mouth."

"Twinkle I need you not to kiss anyone just give hugs. Do you hear me Twinkle, for now on just hugs and handshakes." Diamond continued, "I'm so baffled, how do you go on a date with oh boy and our whole conversation wind up about Sly.

The dude you didn't go on the date with. Twinkle I don't understand your logic. I will encourage you to stick with Jesus, anyone or anything outside of Jesus is no good for you. Your personality is to extreme and there are no gray area's in your life.

However, I'm so glad you slapped the mess out of him because I wanted to break Sly's face."

"Sis when I slapped him he screamed like a … before I could finish."

Diamond said, "A kitchen b!@#$#."

"Yasss." In a whiny tone I asked, "Diamond could she bring Anisa home? And while you are on your way can you get me a cheesesteak with fried onions, lite mayo with extra cheese, cheese fries, a butterscotch krimpet Tasty Kake and a Gingerale from Gaetano's."

"Well damn sis, you are asking for a lot."

"I know, but I need to eat. I'm going to order my food so it will be ready when you get there."

"Alright."

"Thanks Sister."

"Your welcome, Anisa and I will be there shortly."

I got out of my bed, started moving around and splashed some water on my face. My cell phone rang again. It's ten o clock I know Sly is not calling me because this is his time when that "devil oil" is in his system flowing real good.

"Hello."

"Hello Lady."

"Hi Asurion."

"I was checking on you to make sure you were okay."

"I'm okay… thanks for calling, but why are you calling so late?"

Asurion sounding solemnly sorry, "Twinkle I apologize for the lateness of the hour. I wanted to hear your voice before I went to sleep."

Brushing him off, I replied, "That's sweet, thank you and goodnight."

"Goodnight."

My doorbell is ringing, it's Diamond. I opened the door and Anisa ran to me with open arms, "Mommy I missed you," she said as she hugged me tight.

"I missed you too Honeybun."

"Here is your food sis."

"Good look sis, my stomach is hitting my back."

Diamond responded, "And your breath smells like doo doo pebbles."

"Whatever *Booski*. Anisa does mommy's breath stink?"

"Mommy it smells hot."

Slightly embarrassed, asked Anisa, "What does hot smell like."

Innocently she responded, "Onions."

"Honeybun that's not my breath you smell. You smell this cheesesteak because I have fried onions on it."

Anisa gave me a smile like whatever you say Mommy.

Diamond being comedic, "Anisa your mom knows her breath stinks she is just in denial. Twinkle you drunk that liquid poison and your body had an allergic reaction."

"Okay sis."

"I'm just trying to help you out and make sense out of why your breath is hummin' like that."

I ignored her. "Come on Anisa and get ready to go to bed." Anisa washed her face, brushed her teeth and put on her pajamas. I tucked her in the bed.

"Mommy did you speak to my brother."

"No, why do you ask?"

"When my brother was at the house earlier he was looking at my dad like he was mad at him."

"Why would your brother be angry at your dad?"

"I don't know Mommy, but he left out right after you left."

I remembered Shaquan saying he wanted to talk to me about something I thought to myself.

"Baby don't worry about your brother I'm sure he is fine. Let's say our prayers, after we were done we gave each other a hug, kiss and said goodnight."

"Goodnight Mommy."

I quietly shut her bedroom door and walked into the kitchen.

"Diamond thank you so much for picking up my food."

"Twinkle I'm not staying long, I just got a text and I'm about to get in some trouble," following a devious chuckle. "Twinkle I want you to know this."

"What do you want me to know Diamond?" I asked being short because I'm trying to enjoy my cheesesteak.

Diamond responded, "Sister um… don't get short with me; remember I bought you the cheesesteak."

"All I asked you Diamond was what did you want me to know?"

"It's your tone Twinkle; you know we understand the unspoken words. You are basically telling me to shut the F- up."

"I am, I'm hungry and this cheesesteak is bangin'."

"I'm glad you admitted it."

Being frustrated, I asked, "What do you want me to know?"

"Sly and that other dude is 12 o clock."

"What! What is 12:00 o clock?"

Diamond replied in a soprano tone, "Cuckoo… cuckoo following a gibberish riddle, tipy ta tipy toe tipy ta ta toe."

I looked at Diamond and asked, "Was that supposed to be funny?"

She replied, "It was funny to me."

"No it was not Diamond you didn't even laugh." Changing the subject, "Diamond did you notice anything odd with Shaquan and Sly?"

"The only thing I thought was strange was Shaquan left right after you did. Why," Diamond asked being concerned.

"I'm not sure."

There was an obstinate moment of silence.

Diamond breaking the silence, "Alright sis I'm out."

"Thanks again sis."

She then walked out of the door.

After I finished eating, I called Shaquan cell.

"What's up Mom?"

"Hey son you good?"

"Yea!"

"Are you coming home tonight?"

"Nah Mom! I'm going to stay over grandma's house."

Mind you my dad lives in the same house with my mom but for some reason my children insist on calling the house "grandma's house." I don't know why they do, they just do.

"Okay, love you and I'll see you tomorrow."

"Love you too mom, I will see you tomorrow at church."

"Okay. Bye!"

I was glad that Shaquan was still going to church. I know I had hurt him by not telling him the truth about his father, I felt like the guilt and shame was killing me inside. Someway I had to forgive myself.

Parents we are not perfect, and when our children grow up they too will make mistakes. It's part of life. There was a disconnect with Shaquan and I. But at the end of the day I'm not going to force myself on him because then it becomes a sick game. What's meant to be will be. Timing is everything. The love I have for him and the love he has for me will eventually heal the wounds. I believe God.

Chapter 9
How Real Are You?

Today is Sunday, when I was getting ready for church. I kept telling the Lord I need a word directly from him. I told God I need help because it felt like my life was falling apart. I started to feel like I was beginning to go back to my old ways.

As Anisa and I were getting dressed her eyes caught my attention, she looked at me and sincerely said, "Mommy I love you and I trust you."

That messed me up. I had enough knowledge to know once I lost her trust I will no longer be able to effectively raise her because she won't believe anything I tell her. Trust was something I was definitely missing from my parents and I pray I don't lose my children's trust.

Families become disconnected and damaged, because some parents are constantly lying on or to their children because of their deep rooted issues.

One thing I do believe is the truth will always prevail. God got me. I felt like if I go back I will lose her trust and break her heart. Sly has already done that. I went into the bathroom and started praying and crying because I only want the best for my children.

God I need you to fix this. My children are dealing with anger and rejection because of my bad choices concerning the type of men I chose to be their fathers. Which is the same thing I used to battle with; concerning both of my parents, generational curses are real.

It's sad, but the truth is some people demonstrate love through abuse, manipulation, mind games and lies. That is not love. Love changes you for the better, not the worse. Some people are happy being miserable and happier when they make you miserable.

Real love is more peace than drama, if someone is constantly hurting you in a relationship and you keep going back. You need to ask yourself what's keeping you there? The answer is not love. The answer is self-hate.

The truth is; it's easier to stay than to leave. As a parent you have a responsibility to protect your children and not expose them to abuse. Emotional abuse is worse than physical abuse according to psychologist.

Now back to the story. Anisa noticed that I was crying when I walked out of the bathroom. "Mommy are you okay?"

"Yes baby, Mommies allergies are just acting up."

At this time Anisa was at the kitchen table eating Frosted Flakes. I grabbed a bottle of water and an Apple Cinnamon Nutri Grain bar and told Anisa to finish up because we have to leave in a few minutes.

"I'm almost done Mommy," she said while drinking the milk from her cereal.

Smiling I said, "Okay."

We arrived at church, Christ Like, under the leadership of Bishop David C. Glover and his wife, Pastor Kandice Glover. I was a little late so by the time I got there Praise and Worship had already begun.

Why was the praise team singing *Conqueror* from the TV series Empire's episode? *Conqueror* was sung by Jussie Smollett and Estelle on Empire. I really enjoyed the song on Empire. However I was surprised the praise team was singing it.

My church band is awesome. They will usher you right into the holy of holies. I love praise and worship. That is the time I give everything to the Lord. I started to get emotional because I was reminded through the song, *Conqueror,* that I am more than a conqueror through Christ Jesus and so are my children according to the scripture.

However, I still was hurt that my children didn't have better fathers. I pondered, how can a grown man sleep at night knowing their children are hurting?

How can a grown man be emotionally abusive to their children? What kind of man will deliberately hurt their children and play mind games.

God please heal their precious hearts. Bless them and when you do I pray they will be whole and blessed and not broken.

I pray my children will deal with their issues in a healthy way. Jesus please protect my children's emotions and God show them you are their ultimate father their Heavenly father the best father anyone can have.

Heavenly father show them you are their identity and not their bum fathers. Jesus I pray as a mother I will make better decisions for my children. I pray I don't make decisions out of hurt, shame or guilt. I pray for wisdom and that my decisions will help them and not hurt them.

Please don't let my sins or their fathers' sins affect them. God please don't allow my babies to suffer because of my sins. I pray if anyone suffers it will be me.

Right then, I heard God speak and said, "Daughter suffer not. You or your children will not suffer. I have forgiven you and although you don't see a way out, trust me.

My child you are much greater than your circumstances. You are not a victim and neither are your children. You all are victorious. Remember all things work together for the good of them who love the Lord."

Tears started flowing down my face, God help me and give me strength. Right then I realized Praise and Worship was over and they were saying the announcements. I was so caught up I had zoned out.

Mind you I was standing up with my hands lifted up and praying out loud the entire time. I started to wonder after I sat down was I disrupting the announcements? Well if I did Oh, well!

My relationship with God is real and very personal. Shortly after I sat down the Bishop came to the pulpit. He opened up in prayer and stated the title of his sermon is "Forgiveness."

He followed up with how real is your relationship with Christ? He continued, "Fearful and prideful people resist forgiveness to avoid looking weak. But the reality is they are very weak. Forgiveness is a sound decision to let go of resentment and the thought of revenge.

You can forgive the person without excusing the act. Forgiveness doesn't mean you deny the other person's responsibility for hurting you nor does it minimize or justify the wrong. However forgiveness brings a peace that helps you move forward in life.

If you don't forgive, what you are holding on to, it will eventually begin to torture you. When you continue to rehearse the offense you are literally self-destructing yourself. You are letting the devil steal your joy. You are allowing Satan (spiritual enemy) to rob you.

He is robbing your peace, love, joy and happiness. Again, I ask, how real are you? Real people are honest people. They realize at times they get weak, but in your weakness God's strength is made perfect. Honest people don't rationalize their actions so they don't have to forgive. Honest people confront the issue and not avoid it. Now don't get me wrong forgiveness is not easy or quick but you can't allow it to take root in your life.

Forgiveness is difficult because it's unselfish, it involves laying down strong feelings and rights while releasing the other person from his obligation to repay you. God said vengeance is his not revenge. The reason why God said vengeance is his because he already knew what was going to happen to you before you did.

God does not have to re- anything. God is a wise God. The people who hurt you are weak. So if you're expecting the offender to apologize you might be waiting forever or a very long time.

Hurt people make excuses, hurt people lie, hurt people go into denial, hurt people point the finger, hurt people will literally act like the incident never happened and will try to make you feel like everything is your fault. Hurt people will try to hurt you so you can become hurt just like them.

Break through the obstacle of forgiveness so God can bless you. If you have a hard time forgiving, reflect on the times you hurt someone and they forgave you. Don't sit here in this sanctified church and act like you ain't ever hurt anybody.

Be honest with yourself and rebuke that disease called denial and you can't re-call." The congregation started to laugh and little. The Bishop continued, "Most importantly you have to forgive yourself so you can be able to forgive others. Everything starts with you first. Stop looking at everyone's faults so you can avoid your own.

In closing Matthew Chapter 6 verse 15 states, but if you do not forgive others of their sins, your Father in heaven will not forgive your sins. Now forgiveness doesn't mean you are best friends it just means that you let it go and now you're moving forward without them.

Anyone who hinders you or distracts you is not God sent. The people that God sends into your life will push you closer to God and not away from him." Before service was over Bishop asked did anyone need to get saved.

A charcoal in complexion attractive young lady walked to the alter to get saved. This female was on the thin side around 5'4 and she looked like she had a rough life, but she also appeared to be tired of it.

The Bishop said, "Now church we all are going to repeat the sinner's prayer with this young lady. Father, I'm a sinner and I'm sorry for all of the wrong I have done. I ask you to forgive me from all of my sins. I believe you sent your son, Jesus, to die on the cross for me. I believe on the third day he rose with all power and might. I believe if I confess with my mouth and believe in my heart I'm saved. I am now saved in Jesus's name. Amen."

After service, I introduced myself to the young lady because I'm over the women's ministry.

"Hello, my name is Twinkle what is your name," I asked her with a welcoming approach.

"Jelly," she said while rolling her eyes.

'Jelly,' I repeated her name because I was taken back by her name.

She responded, "Yes Jelly is my name," she continued what you don't understand English.

This chick got the game twisted and a real chip on her shoulder. She really don't know about me. I'm like Paul in the Bible. I will go all the way in her mouth and ask God for forgiveness later. I kept saying to myself calm down Twinkle. Father please forgive her because she knows not what she is doing.

Instead I responded, "Obviously I do understand English if I'm here speaking to you.

Jelly look I respect the guard you have up, but real talk I introduced myself to you in peace. I actually like the name Jelly... it's cute."

She began to loosen up a little, "My real name is Kimberly but everyone knows me as Jelly."

"Cool, Jelly here is my number if you want to talk or if you need a ride somewhere just hit me up. I'm out of work for a few months so I have nothing but time."

She snatched the paper and said, "Alright" as she walked away.

I wanted to snatch her neck so bad and ask her did anyone teach her any manners. I said God please don't have this girl call me unless you want me to beat her behind.

Sometimes you have to punch the demons out of people and then pray for them while they are passed out. It's called, "Punch and Pray." Remember, "Punch and Pray." Now don't forget to pray for them after you knock them out.

When I walked outside of the church I heard Shaquan yelling Mom! At first I didn't see him. Then I saw him waving while sitting in his car in the church parking lot. I walked over to him.

"Hey son, what's up?"

"Nothing."

"I'm glad to see you this morning."

"Thanks mom."

But he was really saying whatever mom. You know mothers have that gift. We can read our children's thoughts.

"Mom did you cook?"

"Yea!"

"What did you cook?"

"Come over and find out."

"Okay Mom, I will be there in a few."

Chapter 10
It's Hot

When I arrived home I was in good spirits, however I noticed it was very hot in my place. I checked my central air and it was on, but it wasn't working. I was glad I cooked the night before. It felt like Africa in my house. My God, it was so hot I opened all of the windows.

A few minutes later Anisa nose started to bleed due to the heat. I started to get overwhelmed because my children and I don't do well in the heat. After I took care of Anisa I called my handy man.

"Hello," he answered in his Jamaican accent.

"Hey Haywood!"

"How are you dear?"

"My central air is broke."

"Oh! Dear," he replied.

"Can you come and look at it?"

"Twinkle I'm in Texas and will be back in Jersey in two weeks."

"Haywood what are you doing in Texas?"

"I have a few jobs my dear."

"Okay, I'll just call PSE&G and see what they say."

"Do you still love me?"

Haywood was always flirting with me.

I responded, "Yep, like a brother."

We both snickered and said "good bye."

Anisa knocked on my bedroom door, and then opened it. "Mommy my brother is here."

"Okay, y'all can start eating. I'm trying to take care of something."

"Okay, Mommy," she said while closing my door.

Jesus I need my central air fixed. I want to have a graduation party for Shaquan and now my air is broke. I called PSE&G emergency hotline and told them my situation.

The male customer representative told me I'm no longer on the worry free program due to my late PSE&G payments. He continued, "Your worry free program was terminated, so if you want a technician to come to your residence you will have to pay two- hundred and fifty dollars upfront. And after they diagnose the problem you are going to have to pay whatever it is addition too."

To whoever is reading this, it's going to get better. Remember God will make away. Trust him.

I told PSE&G I will call them back. When I walked out of the room into the living room, my children noticed I was overwhelmed.

"Mom you good," Shaquan asked being caring.

"Yea, I am."

"Mom this steak, broccoli, mac n cheese and cornbread is hitting for something."

Anisa co- signed, "You got that right brother."

I'm glad y'all are enjoying the dinner. I sat down on the couch and begin to watch a lifetime show. After Anisa was done eating she walked into my room.

This is the set up, I know my children. Shaquan wants to tell me something. As soon as I heard the door shut I asked Shaquan what's up.

"Mom it's hot in here."

"Nah duh! I know it's hot in here but that is not what you have to tell me."

"Mom I'm feeling some type of way about Sly."

"Why, what did he do?"

"Him and I betted on a game, I won and he never paid me."

"That's why you are mad at Sly? Didn't he just give you money not too long ago?"

"Yea!"

"So why are you trippin'," I continued, "Didn't I raise you not to make bets? Let this be a learning lesson because people get funny when it comes to money."

"Sly stung me," Shaquan said while raising his voice.

"Why are you surprised he has never been the honest type? If the shoe had been on the other foot Sly would have demanded his money from you."

"Mom, Sly is so grimy."

"I know that is the reason why I don't mess with him."

"Mom your new dude is shady too."

"Shaquan you are just mad."

"I am mad, but that does not change the fact that I love you and want the best for you."

"True, I love you too Son."

"The message in church really touched me it had me thinking about forgiveness;" Shaquan continued, "I was really angry at you. But the truth is; if my biological dad was around I would have known the truth sooner. Thanks Mom for trying to protect me. I know you love me and Anisa.

Just like you want the best for us, we want the best for you. Mom, I'm aware it is the parent responsibility to reach out. You have always bent over backwards for me and I'm sorry for being so angry at you."

"Son you had every right to be angry. Just like you were mad at me, I was mad at myself for making such a messed up decision. Son, I'm still living and learning. I thank God for you." Shaquan gave me a hug. Changing the subject, "I want to have a graduation party for you at Mikado's."

"When Mom?"

"I was thinking, being that you are graduating on Friday – 6/15. I want to have the party on Saturday – 6/16. I'm so excited to know after you graduate, two weeks later you will be going to basic training."

Shaquan smiled.

"Are you nervous son?"

"Just a little bit. Mom what are you going to do about the air?"

"I'm not sure.'"

"Mom today is the first day of June and it's only going to get hotter. I have some money. I'm going to go to Walmart and buy you a window air conditioner to hold you over until you figure something out."

"Thanks Son, I appreciate it."

"No problem. You know Anisa and I suffer from nose bleeds when it's too hot."

"I know."

I called Anisa. "Yes mommy," she replied.

"Your brother and I are done talking." Before Shaquan left, I gave him some money to get two fans.

"Mommy what did you and my brother talk about?"

"None of your business, however he is going to get a window air conditioner and put it in the kitchen window."

While Shaquan was at the store, Anisa and I watched TV and ate a lot of ice. When Shaquan arrived he walked in with a Sunpen town WA -1211 s energy window air conditioner, he put the air conditioner in the window.

Shortly after, the living room started to feel cool.

With pride, Shaquan said, "This air conditioner cools, dehumidifies and vents. Its 12,000 BTU's of power. Basically it should cool the entire kitchen and living room combined with the fans."

Shaquan was always good in math and he is very intelligent.

"Thanks son for everything."

"You're welcome; I'm going over my girlfriend's house I will talk to you later."

As the night went on, I thanked God for resolve and I thanked him for blessing me in spite of my mistakes. So many people are blessed but because their spirit is broken they cannot fully enjoy the blessing. As a result they are not satisfied. Being blessed is a state of mind and not what you have.

They're so many millionaires dealing with drug addiction, suicide and suffer from depression. They don't have peace of mind because they depend on things and people to make them happy.

The ultimate happiness and peace comes from the man upstairs. Many believe in God but believing in him is not enough. You must love and trust him.

Chapter 11
Crazy

Today is Monday; after I got Anisa off to school I chilled for a few. I called Pricy because I kept thinking about her, plus I wanted to tell her about Shaquan's graduation party.

Pricy didn't pick up, so I left her a voice mail message. Although Pricy did me dirty, she still is my cousin and I really love her. Truthfully, I really want the best for her. I know some of y'all are saying F- Pricy and you are right. I'm forgiving her. Bang! Bang! Bang! Gotcha!!!

Not before long, my cell rings. I pick it up and it's Asurion. I answer with an attitude. He just messes up my feng shui.

"Hello, Beautiful."

"Hi Asurion. I'm on another call and I will call you back later."

"Who are you talking to?" he questioned.

"Excuse me, the last time I checked, my phone bill was in my name."

He tried to laugh it off. "My bad Twinkle, I was only playing with you."

"Well the joke is on you and I'll talk to you later."

Asurion hung up the phone. Around 12:30p.m. My doorbell rings. I looked through the peephole and ask who is it?

The man responded delivery. I opened the door and the deliveryman was holding an edible fruit basket. He gave it to me and told me to have a nice day. I replied, "thank you" and closed the door.

When I unwrapped the package it was chocolate covered strawberries dipped in white and milk chocolate. The arrangement was beautiful and the strawberries looked scrumptious.

The card that came with the arrangement read, "One day." I smiled and mumbled to myself, "I must have slapped some good sense into Sly. Because "one day" he really thinks he is going to get some. Let him keep thinking, then instantly I got angry and said this dude is pathetic."

I threw the arrangement in the garbage. Ain't nobody beat for the bull. I wanted to call him so bad and tell him to go suck on some chocolate puddin' pops and leave me the hell alone.

A few minutes later, my doorbell rings again, I looked through the peephole and it was Asurion. *This dude just doesn't give up. What does he want?*

I opened the door and before I could say anything, he forced his way into my house and sits on my couch. This dude is really trying to take my kindness for my weakness. He really doesn't know about the girl Twinkle.

In an authoritative tone he asked, "Where are the edible arrangements?"

I acted like I didn't know what he was talking about. I followed up with, "What is that?"

Aggravated he responded, "I had a fruit basket delivered to you."

I looked at him and calmly replied, "Asurion I didn't get anything."

He stood up so enraged that his cell phone fell out of his pocket.

He screamed, "Twinkle stop testing me, you are just like the others."

I yelled back, "No! You stop testing me and don't come back to my house again."

Asurion stormed out of my house. I slammed the door and locked it. I picked up his phone and looked in his phone history. In his phone history it was nothing but porn site's, but these particular porn sites were violent. It was more like men raping women.

The sex crimes were brutal and then he had porn where the women were defecating on men. It was bizarre and disgusting.

This sick psycho is 730 on a whole other level. And to top it off the only number he had in his phone was my number. Suddenly a feeling of eeriness overtook me.

I started praying with authority, I said, "God has not giving me the spirit of fear but of love, peace and a sound mind."

But real talk I was shook. I called Diamond and told her what happened she started laughing and said, "I knew that cat was crazy. That dude eye was cock eyed looking like can I get a Caesar salad. I read him like I was reading a dirty novel, no pun intended sis." Diamond laughed some more.

"Diamond this is not funny this is serious."

"Twinkle stop trippin' he just like that kinky S&M stuff," she continued, "If you wasn't delivered you probably would be down with it too. Twinkle you are still crazy it's just justified. Get your mind right and give that crazy fool back his phone."

"Diamond this dude is off."

"Twinkle the whole world is," she responded nonchalantly. "Calm down, talk to Jesus and relax. I got to get back to work."

Before Diamond hung up she sarcastically said, "Your life always includes J&D."

"What's J&D?"

Diamond responded, "*Jesus and Drama* it never fails with you. Thank God Jesus will never fail you. Goodbye sis!"

"Bye!"

After we hung up I decided to call the FedEx 1-800 number. When I called I kept getting bounced around. The customer service representative stated they couldn't find him in the system.

Then thirty minutes later, I asked could I speak with a supervisor. Eventually a supervisor answered the call, "Ma'am we don't have anyone by that name who is employed with FedEx."

"Sir," being frustrated responded, "Yes you do."

I repeated Asurion's name and told him he delivered a package to my house a couple of weeks ago. Although he didn't I needed an answer.

"Ma'am, Asurion is not employed at FedEx anymore."

"Why not?"

"I can't disclose the reason, be careful he said with sincerity."

I called Pricy back because I just needed to talk to someone. Pricy picked up, "What Twinkle."

"Come again Pricy, that's how you answer the phone now?"

"I'm busy."

"Well why did you pick up the phone?"

"Because I saw you called earlier."

Pricy's energy was nasty so I decided just tell her about Shaquan's graduation party.

"Is Sly going to be there?"

With my energy being just as nasty as hers, "Why do you ask?"

"Whatever Twinkle," then she banged on me.

I wanted to call her back and tell her off so bad. Pricy has the brazenness to be angry with me. When she was sleeping with Sly for years and I'm still inviting her to family functions like a dummy.

It is funny how people do you wrong and because of their own guilt they treat you like you did something wrong. I call it nugatory reverse psychology. The guilty will always try to make you feel guilty.

Real talk Pricy can kiss my behind. I shouted out loud, "Lord I'm operating in forgiveness," now screaming "Lord I'm trying to operate in forgiveness." But I really wanted to drive to Camden and beat her down. But is she worth it? No.

There is no future in frontin' when it comes to Jesus he really knows how you are really feeling anyway. The truth will make you free and I'm trying to remain free. This might be too real for some but that is not my problem. Let's continue with the story.

Chapter 12
Unexpected Phone Calls

Next week Shaquan will be graduating from high school and I'm super excited. However, I'm a little upset that Greg is in jail and he is not going to be at Shaquan's graduation. Am I surprised? No, I'm not surprised at all. He was never there for him in the beginning so why would he be here now?

I learned the best way to predict someone's future behavior towards you, is to remember their past behavior towards you. Humans - the majority of time are creatures of habit. Honestly, I think its best Greg stays away.

One thing I know, I can't control a grown man. Greg knows that Shaquan is his son and if he really wanted to be there for Shaquan he would have. He would have made all the necessary effort to do so. I don't believe in forcing children to reach out to their fathers or mothers. If you have to force yourself on anyone then those individuals are not meant to be in your life. And clearly that person really does not want to be in your life.

If you make your child reach out, you are setting you child's heart up to be broken. It is not the child's place to teach their parent how to be a parent. After all, it's the parent's responsibility to make sure his or her child is okay. Single mothers / fathers I understand the struggle. Some of us don't want to involve the courts by getting child support because we think if we do, then the fathers / mothers are definitely not going to be involved in the child's life because of anger. But the fact of the matter is; if you have to go there, they weren't going to be involved anyway.

However, sometimes children need closure with their absent parent. I believe closure is needed so the child can move on and never look back.

I started to make phone calls to family and friend's concerning Shaquan's graduation. I called Aunt Hortez to tell her, although she lives in Maine. I just wanted to let her know, what was going on as far as the graduation is concerned.

I wouldn't dare tell my Aunt about Pricy and Sly.

Pricy and Aunt Hortez mother and daughter relationship has always been strained and for some reason they could never mend their relationship.

Aunt Hortez was surprised and excited to hear from me, she stated, "Twinkle I will not be able to make the graduation party however I will send something for you and Shaquan through FedEx.

I'm proud of you Twinkle for raising such a fine young man."

"Aww! Thanks Auntie. I appreciate your well wishes."

"Niece, single mothers are often overlooked. Remember, I was a single mother and it was not easy. But with God on your side he will continue to give you the wisdom and strength."

"Thanks Auntie for the words of encouragement."

"Your welcome sweetheart and your Aunt loves you."

"I love you too."

"Bye baby! Talk to you soon."

I started to feel better. My Aunt was a pistol back in the day; she surrendered to God and did a complete 180 turnaround. I don't know why my Aunt moved to Maine, but to each its own.

I left Asurion's phone on, hoping he would call it. My mind was definitely made up; I was not messing with him anymore.

As I started to prepare dinner, my cell phone rang, I didn't recognize the number but I answered anyway. I was hoping it was one of my family members RSVP to the invite.

"Hello."

"Is this Twinkle?"

"Yes, who is this?"

"Jelly."

"Oh what's up?" *This chick really called.* "Are you okay Jelly?"

"No not really."

"What's wrong?"

"My car broke down and I wanted to know if you can take me food shopping sometime this week?"

"Sure, what day?"

Jelly responded, "Thursday."

"Alright cool, where do you live?"

"Trenton, N.J. in the projects called Trauma."

"Trauma I repeated, what made you move to the worst projects in Trenton? Someone dies there every day."

With an attitude, Jelly responded, "Because they had available housing."

"Do you have children?" I thought changing the subject would be the best thing to do.

"Yes, but do to my lifestyle they are living with my Mom. I got caught up in some stuff and DYFS got involved," Now sucking her teeth Jelly continued. "I can't stand DYFS."

I was just about to tell her I worked for DYFS but decided not to say anything. Because I didn't want her looking at me like I was the enemy. The vibe I caught from her already let me know she really didn't care for me.

"Jelly do me a favor and text me your address."

"I will!"

"Okay, I will pick you up around 10:30 in the morning on Thursday."

"Peace," she said as she hung up.

I see right now, I'm going to have to check this girl early. Now let me be real, Cinnaminson, N.J. is about a thirty to thirty-five minute ride to Trenton. I'm on disability because I'm recovering from double pneumonia and my money is funny right about now.

This girl already has a nasty attitude, but I'm trying to do the Godly thing. Furthermore, I offered and sacrificing my time is part of ministry. When you bless someone God will bless you back. But God knows I'm not feeling this girl.

I asked God to help me conduct myself in the right spirit. Because when you do the right thing in the wrong spirit it's called being phony plus it's a sin. Phony I'm not and sinful I don't want to be. I want my motive and deed both to be genuine.

My cell rings again. I said to myself, I just can't get a break.

It's my mom and my mom never calls me. She probably is responding back to the message I left her about Shaquan's graduation party.

"Hey Mom!"

"Hello Dear. I received your message about Shaquan's graduation party. Do you need me or your father to help you with anything?"

"I'm okay Mom. But I do need to ask you and Dad a question so could you put the phone on speaker." The phone is now on speaker.

"Mom and Dad why didn't you tell me Shaquan is staying at your house?"

My Mom responded, "Because I thought you knew."

"Did you ever wonder or care how I thought about it?"

My Dad responded while his voice being elevated, "You should have called. Twinkle I didn't know what was going on."

"Okay, so why didn't anyone call me to ask me what was going on?"

My Dad said, "Because we don't have to because this is my house."

My Mom follows up with, "Why do we have to call you and ask you anything, we are Shaquan's grandparents."

"My sentiments exactly, I feel like you and Dad never support me and you two always overstep your boundaries. It hurts and it's not right."

My Dad responds, "Twinkle you always want a pity party."

Before I could respond, my Mom replied, "Twinkle we didn't call to argue with you and every time I speak to you I get a headache. Your father and I will see you at the graduation."

I was hurt when the call ended but I should be use to it for the simple fact this is how I was raised.

Oh well, life goes on right. I shook it off and continued with my day. My cell rings again. It felt like the calls were non- stop.

"Hey sister," Diamond said while sounding chipper.

"Hey Diamond!"

"Twinkle I have to tell you something."

"Okay what is it?" I paused… "Hold on Diamond, Shaquan is calling on the other line."

"Hey Son!"

"Mom!"

"Yes." I answered.

"I forgot what I was about to tell you."

I thought that was odd.

"Okay, when you remember call me back. I have Aunt Diamond on the other line." I clicked back over.

"Alright sis, I'm back. Diamond I just got off the phone with your parents."

Although they are both of our parents this is how we address them to one another.

"I told them how I felt about Shaquan staying over there and I told them how I was hurt." My nose started to tingle and I began to cry a little.

Diamonds said, "Sis count to ten and get a tissue."

I sniggered. "Enough about me, what did you have to tell me?"

"I'm good sis you have enough on your plate and I don't want to overwhelm you with my issues. Twinkle, Diamond said in a rushed whisper, my boss is walking toward my cubicle. I will call you later."

What it is going on, I yelled out loud. My son and my sister are holding something back from me. Okay, I'm just going to act like I don't know anything.

Sometimes it's better to act like you don't know what's going on until the time is right. Ask God to give you the gift of discernment if you don't already have it. Also ask God for wisdom, knowledge, but most of all understanding. Double minded people will tell you what you want to hear but do the total opposite of what they said. As a result you will become confused.

Double-minded people will always operate in drama. You know why? Because a double minded man / woman is unstable in all of their ways.

Anytime you are confused about anything the majority of time two major components are missing, which is honesty and clarity. The author of confusion is satan and he is the father of all lies. Be mindful of people who operate in constant drama.

Chapter 13

Some ish

Anisa woke me up early in the morning because her nose was bleeding. It was very hot and uncomfortable in my condo. I shouted "God; I need my central air fixed."

Today is Thursday I texted Jelly to make sure she still wanted me to take her food shopping. I really didn't want to take her because I was hot and aggravated.

Jelly texted me back, "yea."

"C u at 10:30," I texted back.

I started to get myself together and drove to her place of residence.

I texted Jelly, "I' m here."

When I pulled up it was like every other project. People were outside smoking weed; drinking and some were walking and talking to their self. A few guys walked passed my car and winked at me. I just looked at them.

You had some neighbors looking out there window to see who I was there for. Everybody in the hood is not bad. There is a lot of great talent in the hood however because of the lack of guidance it's not able to come to fruition.

There comes a time when your mindset has to change and your character has to align with your gift. If this does not happen then you are going to stay stuck, and it doesn't matter where you are from. That's a universal law. A successful mindset knows its self-worth. A mature mindset will allow you to navigate and network effectively. If you have the mindset that everybody owes you something or you are supposed to get something for nothing. You are going to stay right where you are, and that is broke.

In order to make money you have to give money and that begins with giving to God, investing into self and to others. God gives seed to the sower.

Finally Jelly comes outside walks to the car and shouted, "It's hot as hell out here."

I responded, "This heat right here is called *you better get right heat*. It reminds me that hell is a place that I don't want to go."

Jelly responded, "Shit and then quickly said my bad."

"It's cool Jelly. What market am I taking you too?"

"Bottom Dollar, its only fifteen minutes away."

Thank God.

"Twinkle can we stop by 711 it's on the way, I want a Blueberry Slurpee."

I gave her a look like its 10:30a.m. You should have got your Slurpee before I got here.

"Which way am I going Jelly?"

She began to direct me and the 711 was literally around the corner. When I pulled up to 711, I thought about it. A Blueberry Slurpee does sound good. Jelly got out of the car first.

Right before I was about to get out. Diamond called me and said she really has to tell me something.

"Sis, let me call you right back."

Right then I saw Buf walking out of the 711 she got so huge that her butt blended in with her back.

She yelled, "Twinkle is that you."

"Yea, it's me."

"What you doing out here?" she said as she walked towards my car.

"Buf shouldn't I be asking you that question, you are the one from Philly."

"Gurl" she responded, "I moved to Jersey for a change of scenery."

Brushing her off, "It was nice seeing you Buf."

"Twinkle the day I came to your grandmother's funeral I was on some other stuff I was young and stupid."

"Gurl you good, we both were on some immature stuff."

I got out of my car to give her a hug. As she walked away, you would never believe who was walking out of the 711.

The boy Sly. Really? Buf and Sly is back messing with each other again. Ain't this some ish. Sike!!!

It was Asurion.

Whew, I crack my own self up. This dude walked out of 711 lighting a cigarette and didn't even notice me.

"What's up Asurion," I said as I walked towards him.

"Oh! Twinkle! What you doing out here?"

I ignored his question and responded, "I thought you lived in Ewing."

"I do but I had to deliver a package."

Mind you this dude is not in his uniform nor is he driving the FedEx truck. In matter of fact this dude is on foot. But I'm just going to act stupid.

"I'm glad I bumped into you because your phone is at my house."

"I was looking all over for my phone."

"Well it's at my house."

"Can I get it today?"

"Today is not a good day."

"How about Friday?"

"Friday is good but you have to come no later than 11:00 in the morning, because I have to run errands."

"Twinkle I will be at your house at 9:00a.m. Because I have off of work."

I said, "Okay like I didn't know he was no longer working for FedEx."

I walked into 711 and purchased my Slurpee. Jelly was in 711 talking to some of her home-girls. Now we are back in the car.

While I'm driving to Bottom Dollar, Jelly asked, "Twinkle how do you know the 'Gager?'"

"Who is the 'Gager'?"

"The dude you were just talking to at 711."

Curiously, I asked, "Why do you call him the Gager?"

"He is psycho Twinkle."

"Jelly and so am I, as I shook my head like what."

"Twinkle did you know he sleeps with prostitutes?"

"No, I didn't."

"Not only does he sleep with them he doesn't pay them neither. When the girl demands her money he then starts choking her, not until death, but to intimidate her."

"Jelly how do you know?"

"Twinkle when I was on that stuff, I used to trick."

"What stuff was you on Jelly?"

"I smoked dope, crack and weed. I still smoke weed. This is the reason why my kids are in the system because my urine always comes back dirty."

"How old are your children?"

"I have four boys."

"Wow!"

"They are 10, 8, 7, and 3."

"Jelly don't you think you need to stop smoking for your kid's sake?"

"I'm trying but its weed. I'm trying to have my doctor give me a prescription for medical marijuana."

I chuckled a little.

"Twinkle you are a nice lady in church and all. The "Gager" is nobody you want to mess with. He is the devil."

"Jelly that dude ain't built for me on that level. I have God and a Heavenly host that God charges to protect me on a daily. I'm good, trust me."

I started to do inventory on myself. Silently I asked, "God why I attracted a dude that is so evil. Am I that vulnerable and lonely? What is my problem?"

"Twinkle," Jelly shouted, "Make a right. Are you alright Twinkle? I was telling you that you were going to have to make a right in a little while and you didn't respond."

"My bad Jelly my mind was somewhere else."

We are now in the Bottom Dollar parking lot. We got out of the car and Jelly got a cart. I thought to myself I may as well pick up a few things since I'm here. I grabbed a cart too.

While we were food shopping I noticed males and females were walking up to Jelly and giving her love. I could tell that Jelly is popular and well liked in her neighborhood.

I kept overhearing male and females telling Jelly they need some more lessons. *What kind of lessons are they talking about I wondered*? Let me find out Jelly is giving piano lessons in the hood? That's what's up. I promote anything positive. When I was driving Jelly back to her place. I told Jelly I overheard people asking you about lessons.

She responded, "That's good" as if she didn't want to tell me what kind of lessons they were referring too.

So bluntly I asked. "Jelly what kind of lessons do you give?"

"Twinkle I don't think you really want to know."

"Jelly if I didn't want to know, then I would never have asked you. Besides it can't be that bad. I continued, what, are you giving piano lessons?"

Jelly laughed and replied, "Twinkle you been in the church too long." She followed up with you are funny. I looked at her trying to figure out what was so funny.

Being serious, I asked again, "What kind of lessons are they?"

"Gosh, Twinkle," she said while sucking her teeth, "You are so nosey."

"Yes I am. Are you going to tell me?"

Jelly started scratching her head as if she was reluctant to tell me. Finally she said, "Twinkle I'm an oral sex teacher."

"You are an oral sex teacher," I repeated.

"Yea you heard right," Jelly said while being defensive.

"Wait! Hold up!" So many questions started racing through my mind.

"How do you teach people how to perform oral sex? Do you use real people and perform these sexual acts. I'm confused Jelly."

"I don't perform oral sex on people however I demonstrate these acts on fruits, vegetables and toys, such as bananas, carrots and cucumbers."

"So do you teach male and females or just females?"

"I teach both sexes."

More questions started racing through my mind.

"So are you bisexual?"

"I'm a switch hitter."

"What is a switch hitter?"

Twinkle she said in frustration, "I bat both ways. I told you Twinkle that you weren't ready," she said while nodding her head.

"Yea your right Jelly I wasn't." Now since Jelly has opened up to me, she got real comfortable.

"That's how I got my name Jelly."

"How did you get it," curiously I asked?

"My first demonstration was with a peanut butter and jelly sandwich." She went on to say when she put the Jelly on top of the peanut butter.

Quickly, I interrupted, "Jelly I'm good. I don't need to know the details of your demonstration, because I don't want to feel some type of way about peanut butter and jelly sandwiches. How much do you charge for these lessons?"

"One hundred and fifty dollars for a thirty minute session, anything after thirty minutes I charge twenty five dollars in fifteen minutes increments."

"How did you get into this profession?"

"I figured that everyone needs extra help in this area, plus it's legal."

"Jelly its immoral."

"How Twinkle?"

Before I could answer, Jelly said with confidence, "I have the gift to help."

"Jelly, remember the tootsie roll commercial when we were kids. The commercial asked how many licks does it take to get to the middle of the tootsie roll."

"Yea, I remember."

"What I'm trying to say is you can't use the same oral sex technique on everyone for the simple fact that everybody doesn't like the same thing the same way."

Jelly interjected, "You right, it depends on the sex and saliva Twinkle." Jelly continued, "Although the commercial never had an official answer it promoted there brand."

"Jelly your brand needs to be banned because it not legit."

Jelly now being funny, "Twinkle you probably need some lessons because you been out of touch for a while."

"No Boo Boo, I'm celibate because I was touching too much and myself worth and self-respect is priceless."

"Whatever Twinkle!"

"It won't be whatever when stuff start going down the wrong wind pipe and you start choking." I laughed a little.

"Oh, you got jokes Twinkle."

"I sure do, but on the serious note you need a job that doesn't require you tapping into wicked imagination, fantasy and perversion. Being that you enjoy doing things with your mouth, maybe you need to look into becoming an oral pathologist?"

"What's that?"

"An oral pathologist is a dentist that specializes in the research and diagnosis treatment of diseases affecting the oral and maxillofacial regions. They make good money Jelly, real good money. I just believe that will work out better for you in the short and long run.

Jelly the sky is the limit. Don't settle. Being an oral sex teacher has no long- term benefits such as health benefits, pension, 401 k plan, 403B plan or a deferred compensation. You need to think about your future because you have children. Look into an IRA and different investments. Real talk that's how real bosses move. We move wise, we move forward and we know how to count honest money. Jelly you being hood rich, making quick money, collecting SSI or on welfare along with working under the table is not going to last. You need a job with substance. You think you are getting over on the system but actually the system is getting over on you."

"How is the system getting over on me?"

"Jelly you can only go but for so far, you are cheating and limiting yourself, it's called having a slave mentality. Knowledge is power. The Good Book states my people perish do to a lack of knowledge. That's your hustle and frankly I think it's a real creative one, however you need something stable. God wants the best for you because you deserve the best. Work hard now so you can play harder later. Real rap!"

"Jelly responded that's dope. I never had anyone speak positive to me. My mom used to tell me to use what I got to get what I want."

"Jelly, I understand but what you do have is a brain, so use it."

"Thanks Twinkle you are cool peeps."

"So are you Jelly."

I pulled in front of Jelly's door; she started to take her bags out of the trunk of my car.

"Here Twinkle, here is twenty dollars. I appreciate you taking me food shopping."

"Thank you. Are you going to church on Sunday?"

Jelly responded, "Baby steps Twinkle."

I responded; "Well take your baby steps to church on Sunday."

Jelly smiled and said, "Alright."

As I was driving home, I asked God for forgiveness because I really didn't want to take her anywhere because I really didn't like her. Be careful how you treat people because you never know who God will use to save your life.

I can't believe I saw the boy Asurion, this dude is really 730, which is the urban code for crazy. The police code is 5150 for psycho equivalent to a mental patient. This dude is walking around like he is an abiding citizen.

Maybe I should have the police at my house when he comes to get his phone. I just don't trust him because he is a criminal and he is evil. Nah, I'm good if Asurion wants to act like he lost his mind he is going to have a very rude awakening messing with me. I asked Jesus to dispatch my warring angels and angels of protection to protect me and my children, because I don't know who he is and what demon is inside of him.

However I will not live in fear. I started analyzing myself again. Why in the hell did I attract and was attracted to a man that is literally a monster. What spirit is in me? Because real talk I was feeling him at first.

He was "stalker(ish) fine," well at least that is what I thought at first. When I changed my life for the better I came up with a 6-C rule to keep me away from creeps. This rule was to keep me focused. I know y'all are wondering what the 6-C rule is. Calm down I'm about to tell you. (Snickering) I so love my readers.

I also came up with the 4- D.E.V.S which stands for devilish behaviors in a relationship you need to be mindful of. Which are: **D** - Dishonesty in small or large things. **E** - Explosive and unexpected anger while dating. **V** - Violence toward you of any kind. **S** - Sarcasm who's teasing crosses the border into aggression, critical and demeans.

Some of y'all just said this is exactly how my dude acts. If you said this, it might be time for you to re-evaluate your relationship.

Now the 6-C's stand for Christ, Cash, Career, Car, Crib and good Credit, these 6 factors are very important for a productive successful relationship.

So again I'm asking myself why was I feeling Asurion? Was it because he was a new face and I was lonely and vulnerable? Or is it because my faith was starting to dwindle do to me getting weary.

Or is it the fear of being alone for the rest of my life? One thing I'm not going to do is have a pity party. I'm going to ask God for strength, learn from this and continue to trust and love God.

The devil is so crafty he always knows when to show up when you're at your most vulnerable point in your life.

Remember this, when the devil shows up God will always be your present help when you are in trouble. Don't even trip. Don't lose your expectation, because if you do you will lose your miracle.

Chapter 14

Heart to Heart

I finally pulled up to my place put my groceries away and prepared to make baked Ziti for dinner. I turned on the TV, and soon as I sat down my cell phone rang; it never fails.

Sometimes I just want to throw my cell phone of out the window. It was Aunt Hortez.

"Hey Auntie!"

"Hey baby how are you feeling?"

"I'm doing better; I'm breathing a lot better that double pneumonia was no joke."

"I know sweetheart some people die from it."

"I heard, so what's up Auntie?"

Auntie being hesitant, asked have I spoken to Pricy? I was apprehensive to answer because I know that's a set up question meaning she is fishing for information about Pricy.

Auntie I spoke to her not to long ago because I invited her to Shaquan's graduation party.

She responded, "I see."

"Have you spoken to her Auntie?" I said to myself, *I know Pricy did not tell my Aunt that her and Sly was messing around.* My Aunt answer interrupted my thoughts.

"Twinkle I spoke to Pricy the other day, she told me she hates me and her life. Then she hung up the phone.

When I tried to call her back she didn't answer."

"Auntie, why would Pricy say such a thing?"

"Pricy blames me for her drug addiction because I sent her to live with your grandma when she was twelve."

"Auntie, may I ask you why did you have her move with grandma?"

With a deep sigh, "Twinkle your aunt is not the perfect aunt everybody thought I was."

I thought to myself, nobody thought you were perfect that disease called denial is real. But I went along with it like I was clueless.

"What happened Auntie?"

"I don't know why I'm sharing this with you; I guess it's time for me to get free. Hopefully if I do maybe me and Pricy can have the mother and daughter relationship I have always desired." Auntie continued, "As you know your grandparents, which are my parents kept me in church and instilled Christ in me.

Now since you're a woman I feel as though I can share this with you. What I'm about to tell you nobody knows this but your grandparents. Not even your mom knows this. When I was fifteen years old; a married older Deacon used to visit your grandparent's church from time to time and he seduced me. This man was real close to the family so every time we had a family function he was always present.

As a result I got pregnant with Pricy. I wanted to get an abortion but your grandparents didn't believe in abortions. So they made me have Pricy and made me promise not to tell anyone who the father was.

The Deacon was a very wealthy man and he paid them a pretty penny to keep quiet. The secret tortured me to the point the same neighbors Pricy used to get high with. I got high with their mother."

"Wow! I'm sorry to hear this Auntie."

"To this day Pricy doesn't know who her father is and now he is dead."

"Wait! Auntie! You killed him too?"

"Twinkle you are so crazy," she said while laughing. "No, I didn't kill him. He died some years ago from lung cancer. He was a chain smoker. This is the reason why I moved to Maine because I didn't want to be reminded of my past."

"Auntie, grandma always said running away from your problems is a race you will never ever win."

"Niece at times I wish she took her own advice. This is the reason why I had an aught with Jesus for such a long time. I finally realized that Jesus is not who the religious or church folks make him out to be. A lot of these saints are *aints*.

Some thing's need to be exposed so the healing process can begin, so many people are ashamed and embarrassed from their past. This is the reason why parents raise their children in error.

Children are often taught to maintain an "image" so they can impress people who are just as bad or worse than them. Image destroys families, lives and generations. Twinkle the truth hurts but the truth will also make you free.

Please, Twinkle don't get caught up in pleasing people. As long as you continue to please God his blessings will forever be bestowed upon you and your children.

Regardless of your mistakes."

"Thanks Auntie for your words of wisdom and this conversation will stay between you and I."

"Thanks sweetheart, expect your package next week."

"Okay I will. Auntie keep your head up."

"Love you Twinkle and stay authentic, people may hate you for being different and not living by society's standards, but deep down they wish they had the courage to do the same."

"Love you too Auntie."

"Talk to you soon honey."

After the phone call ended I just sat on my couch in shock for a few minutes. I swore to secrecy and I can't tell anybody this crap.

Jesus please help my Aunt, heal her heart and give her the courage to tell Pricy the truth in Jesus name Amen.

Chapter 15
Neighbors

Suddenly my doorbell rung, I looked out of the peephole. When I opened the door my female Caucasian neighbor Holly was crying hysterically and holding her Jack Russell dog.

"Twinkle speaking real fast can I use your phone because Zak and I got into an argument." Holly still speaking fast continued; "While I was walking the dog Zak left and I didn't bring my keys because I didn't think he was going to leave.

Can I come inside Twinkle?"

"With your dog Holly?"

"Twinkle," she said while being flabbergasted, "I don't know where to put him."

Being stern, I responded, "Outside Holly it's a dog."

"What if he runs away?"

"Holly that crying behind dog is not going to go anywhere. Holly he can't come into my house. How about you give me Zak's number, I will call him and put him on the speaker while I stand outside."

"Okay Twinkle… Okay Twinkle."

"Holly calm down you and him are always arguing. Zak ain't going nowhere."

"How do you know Twinkle?"

"You all been living directly above me for 5 years and for 5 years I've been hearing y'all argue every day along with your dog crying and running around the apartment."

"I'm sorry Twinkle; I didn't know you could hear us."

"Yea, Holly I can, every day," followed with a smile.

She looked at me in the state of confusion. Like should I smile back or tell my dog to sic her. Holly decided to give me the evil white girl stare and then she flicked her hair.

I looked at her like I didn't do it and you are at my door. I dialed the number while the phone was ringing. I saw Zak park into his parking spot. Holly there is Zak now.

"Ewwww!!! Douche bag, he's going to get it."

"Bye Holly," I said as I shut my door.

Drama really makes the world go around.

Chapter 16
Baby Sis Is Always Ready

I began to cook my Ziti. I couldn't wait for my baby girl to come home because I knew for sure she was going to have a funny story.

Finally I hear the key juggling in the door. Anisa opens the door. Her bright smile greets me following a hey Mom as she walked over to me to give me a hug.

"Hey Honeybun!"

"Mom it smells good up in here. What are you cooking?"

"Your favorite baked Ziti."

"Yes," Anisa said while being excited. "Mom I'm glad because I'm hungry."

"What did you have for lunch?"

Anisa smile turned into a frown. "I had processed mac and cheese, cold broccoli with no flavor and a stale piece of bread that is hard as a hockey puck. Our school lunch don't be poppin' like that."

I chuckled. "Get settled and start your homework."

"Okay Mommy. Thank God, I don't have a lot of homework and because tomorrow is Friday, I will have no homework," she said as she walked to her room.

After Anisa was done with her homework she helped me fix the Garden Salad that I was preparing for dinner. My baby girl loved to help me cook and I loved her help.

After dinner was done Anisa and I ate and talked about her day some more, I reviewed her homework and watched TV until it was time for her to go to bed. We both went to bed early because we had the itis. In the middle of the night Anisa came in my room.

"Mommy I had a bad dream someone broke into our house and put a bunch of spiders in our house. Mom the spiders were alive and they were everywhere."

"Baby come and sleep in my bed and I will protect you."

I figured she went to bed too early after she ate and that's why she had a bad dream. The next day I got Anisa ready for school we said our prayers then we walked to the bus stop. Before she got on the bus she said, "Mommy remember no weapon formed against us shall prosper."

I smiled and said, "You better know it. Have a wonderful day," I shouted as she got on the bus.

I walked back home and said Jesus give me the wisdom to deal with this Nut that's about to come over to get his phone. I turned on the gospel station to set my atmosphere and to calm my nerves.

I wanted to tap into a sense of peace before he stopped bye. I had to get my mind right. I called my sister to tell her that Asurion was coming over to pick up his phone. Diamond realized I was a little worried and asked, "Where is Shaquan?"

"He is in school," I replied being agitated.

"My bad Twinkle."

"What time is the crazy guy coming over?"

"At 9:00a.m. I told him to come early because I had to run errands."

"Alright, Twinkle I'm on my way just in case this ocelot decides to act up. You know I will shoot him."

"Diamond you are coming over with heat?"

"Yea," she responded as if she was surprised I asked her the question.

"Twinkle we are too old to be fighting, we both are overweight and out of shape plus he is a dude and ain't nobody got time for that. And I still have to go to work so we have to expedite and execute this mission."

"Diamond I just don't think that extreme measures are necessary."

"Sis! What do you suggest being that you have all the answers?"

"Remember the switch I used to threaten Shaquan with."

Diamond interrupted me and said sis, "A switch…
really!!! Twinkle you are buggin'. You are going to beat a
grown man with a switch?"

"Yea, if I have too."

"Okay, Twinkle you beat him while I shoot him."

"Diamond you need to get delivered."

Diamond shouting back, "I will after he gets his
phone. I'm on my way," then she hung up. Diamond
arrived at my house fifteen minutes later. When she walked
into my house she was ready.

"Diamond your energy is too high."

She responded, "Sis no disrespect, but ever since
you got saved you be acting like a punk. Don't the bible
say Heaven suffers violence and the violent take it by
force?"

"Yes," I responded.

"Well sometimes you have to get violent Twinkle."

"Diamond the bible also states a gentle tongue can
break a bone. Let's deal with this dude in a gentle way.
Trust, your sis ain't never been a punk, matter of fact I
taught you what you know and don't forget it baby sis."

Diamond shouting, "Now that's the Twinkle I know,
about that life. Word! I knew you still had it in you."

"Oh! It's still here it's just not my first reaction."

"Well, I'm not there yet sis. But this is your house and I'm going to respect it. I'm not going to shoot unless he gives me probable cause to do so. If I observe anything shifty I'm shooting. No questions."

"Diamond is your gun registered?"

"Yes," Diamond appearing to be annoyed. "Twinkle I am licensed to carry. This dude got a reputation for raping females and the streets calls him the "gager" and you have the audacity to ask me if I'm license to carry. You know what Twinkle you are something else."

Right then my doorbell rings, it was Asurion. I opened the door halfway and gave him his phone while he was standing outside and asked him not to call me anymore. Because the door wasn't open all of the way he couldn't see my sister.

He gave me a dehumanizing stare. I stared at him back like if you know what's best for you. You will leave now and never come back. Creepily he nodded, turned around and walked away. I closed the door.

"Twinkle that dude is a punk."

"Thank God it's over; I pray he doesn't come back."

Being hesitant, Diamond replied, "He's coming back. As bad as I don't want to admit it, the vibe I caught I know he's coming back."

I responded, "The devil might be working hard but he is not working harder than my God."

"True sis! Jesus got you. Twinkle I'm out. I will call you later."

"Thanks Diamond."

After Diamond left I prayed because in my heart I knew Diamond was right. What she felt I was feeling too.

Heavenly Father you gave me the power to tread over serpents, scorpions and most of all the devil. I rebuke the hands of the wicked and every scheme the devil has for my life and my children's life. Cover us with your powerful blood and I pray that no harm will come to my dwelling place in Jesus Name Amen.

Chapter 17

The Package

I decided to take Anisa to Wildwood for the weekend. Anisa loves to swim and this will be a great surprise for her. I need to just getaway and relax.

We arrived in Wildwood Friday, at 6:30p.m. and checked in our room. It felt so good to be at a hotel because the air conditioner was working and I put it on high. Being that we were hungry, we ate at the Star Diner Café they have great food and a relaxed family atmosphere.

Saturday we were at the beach for most of the day and we ate funnel cake, fried Oreo's and ice-cream. Sunday we walked the boardwalk, rode the rides and played games. It was a nice fun filled weekend.

Although I missed church on Sunday we still had a great getaway. On my way home Shaquan called me and asked how I was doing? I told him Anisa and I was coming from Wildwood.

"Oh, that's why you weren't at church. Mom I was checking on y'all making sure you two were okay."

"Aww! Thanks son yea we're good. I just decided to get away for the weekend that's all."

"Is it still hot in the Condo?"

"Yes, and Anisa is still having nose bleeds from time to time but we are making it. I'm going to get the central air fixed soon."

"Mom, you know I'm about to leave in two weeks."

"I know son."

"What are you going to do without me?"

"Shaquan you ain't even been here so what you think I've been doing?" I answered my own questions. "I've been living and raising your sister. You are seventeen, I wish you were here but if you think living with your grandparents is a better atmosphere for you, then so be it.

Regardless you are my son and sometimes to see people for who they are you have to live with them. Son the bond we have is unbreakable."

"Yea, mom we always been close."

"Son now it's your time to live and learn. I'm glad you went to church."

"I left after I paid my tithes."

"I know that's right." We both chuckled.

"I was going to stop by."

"We are just leaving. We won't be home until 5p.m. and besides the only reason why you are calling me is because you thought I cooked." Shaquan laughed a little.

"Alright mom, drive safe and I will see you later. Tell my sister that I love her and I love you too."

"Love you back son."

The next day Anisa didn't want to go to school. Being that she had a fun filled weekend. She had the Monday blues, but she has to go to school. Finally I sent her off to school and now I'm home relaxing.

I called Pricy because I really love and miss my cousin. Although she is a basket case I still miss her. She always had my back and I know she loves me too. Pricy didn't pick up. I believe the guilt is making her stay away from me. When she didn't pick up I said to myself, she will be alright and eventually she will get her mind right.

Suddenly my door rang. When I looked out of the peephole I didn't see anyone. Cautiously, I opened the door; there was a package in front of my door. Instantly, I smiled so hard that I saw my own white teeth being displayed in dazzling rows.

I'm so excited because I know this package is from Aunt Hortez. I grabbed the package and carried it into the house. I sat down on the couch. I opened the package it had cellophane, white balls and bubble sheeting. Everything was cushioned securely. Aunt Hortez is so sweet.

As I moved the cellophane white balls, I saw a note that read, "You are the head and not the tail." Auntie is so loveable and knows how to speak in my life. There were six individual gifts wrapped in newspaper, I figured some were for me and some were for Shaquan. I took one of the gifts out of the package with great anticipation I removed the newspaper. On the radio, Outkast – So Fresh, So Clean was playing. I'm singing the lyrics ain't nobody dope as me I'm just so fresh so clean (So fresh and so clean clean). As I'm removing the newspaper, I'm grooving. When I removed the newspaper I screamed and jumped.

When I jumped up something that appeared to be a gruesome head of a vulture fell out of my hand. I watched it as it rolled across the floor. I yelled, what the…. time stopped for a few seconds. Immediately I looked on the box for the sender's name. There was none. The package just had my address. I can't believe this bird head was stuffed and the skin of the head was mounted.

This has Sly's name all over it. I guess he is a taxidermist. At least he has a job, I said to myself as I walked into the kitchen to pick up the head with a spatula, which I threw the bird head, the package and the spatula in the trash. I took the garbage to the dumpster and called Sly. Surprisingly he picked up.

"Good one Sly."

I guess he was getting me back from the possum, but he is so corny.

Sly screamed, "I told you, you were going to get yours and that's what you get." He continued yelling something I couldn't understand so I banged on him.

Sly is so stupid. I wanted to drive to Philly so bad. But what would be the use? That's what he wants.

I shouted out loud, "Lord my life has to get better. Whatever I'm not learning please let me learn so I can stop repeating the same dysfunctional cycle. In Jesus name amen."

I called Jelly to vent. I couldn't call Diamond because she would black out. Jelly picked up the phone, while fast-talking said, "Twinkle I know I didn't go to church, because I overslept. So don't call me harassing me about it because I will be there next Sunday."

"First of all Jelly, I didn't go myself. So chill regular. I was calling you to tell you about my drama."

"My bad Twinkle, but you know y'all church people can be persistent at times."

"Jelly, hold on someone is beeping my other line."

"Hello," I answered.

"Hello Sweetheart."

"Hey Auntie hold on and let me tell the person on the other line I will call them back. Jelly, I'm going to call you back, this is my Aunt and she is calling from Maine."

"Alright Gurl!"

"Hey Auntie what's up?"

"I'm calling you to let you know instead of me sending you and Shaquan a package. It will be easier for me just to mail both of you all a card with money in it."

"Thank you so much Auntie."

"I already mailed the cards so they should arrive to Jersey no later than Thursday."

"Okay, I'll keep a look out for them. Thanks again, and I will call you when I receive them."

"Okay baby we will talk soon."

"Okay Auntie."

Chapter 18
Regardless I'm Good

A couple days passed. I decided to go to Bottom Dollar because it is going out of business and I heard they had good sales. You know when you are used to working being home can be a bit of a challenge.

Today is Wednesday and in the working world we call it "hump day." The majority of the time there is an excitement because Friday is almost here. I didn't feel excited at all. Looking at the bright side, at least I will be out of work for most of the summer.

When Anisa gets out of school my day will be so much better because we will be taking a lot of day trips. I'm beginning to feel like myself, I'm not 100 percent well but my breathing is getting much better and my lungs are feeling stronger. Thank God.

I got myself together and drove to Bottom Dollar it just felt good to get out of the house. As I'm browsing around the store, I'm checking out all of the sales and enjoying my "me time." Now I'm in the aisle looking for Anisa's Goldfish pretzel snacks and I can't find them anywhere. I see the regular Goldfish and the extra cheddar but not the pretzel. I'm starting to get irritated because those are her favorite and I really don't feel like going to another store to get them.

When I looked up, Asurion said, "Boo" he came out of nowhere while standing right beside me.

I made the hand gesture like I was about to blow him a kiss, instead I replied, "Boohoo baaack to you." I continued, "Asurion I just want you to know that God is the only one that approves of you being his stalker," following a light chuckle.

"Are you shopping Twinkle?"

"Are you," I said as I snapped at him?

"Twinkle where is all of the aggression coming from?"

When I started to walk away he stood in front of my shopping cart. So I stopped and stared at him.

"Don't you want to come over for dinner Twinkle?"

"No, but I do want you to leave me alone."

"Twinkle you are so assertive."

"Asurion what do you want?"

"I want to tell you what I'm cooking for dinner tonight."

Now being agitated I asked, "What are you cooking?"

"I'm glad you asked. I'm making cheese and garlic crack bread, sweet potato casserole with Andouille sausage, baby carrots and my specialty fried turkey vulture."

My angry stare became more defined. "So you are the one who sent me that package."

"Twinkle, Twinkle," he repeated my name in a spooky tone. He continued, "I always knew you were the sharpest knife in the kitchen. I don't know if you were aware of this, but emotions are such a deadly weapon."

"Do you want a cookie Asurion?"

"Perhaps I do. Preferably from Chick-fila, those chocolate chip cookies are to die for," he said as he chuckled.

"I got right in his face and said if you come for me, be prepared to get your ass beat."

He sniffed me and said, "Twinkle your fragrance always smells so lovely."

"And you Asurion always smell like produce junction."

"Twinkle, that is the garlic you smell. I heard garlic keeps the vampire's away," he said while looking mischievous.

"And my sweet savory smells keeps the demons away," I smiled. "Asurion now go home and cook your damnable dinner and enjoy it by yourself."

As I walked away he said, "My dinner is going to be devilishly delicious."

His voice now becoming elevated said, "Twinkle you need to learn how to get out of your feelings."

I ignored him and continued to walk away. Now Asurion is yelling in the middle of the aisle, "My dinner is a delicacy Twinkle it's a damn delicacy."

I continued food shopping. Ain't nobody stutin' that nut. I went from one nut to another.

That's why it is so important to wait on God ladies and gentlemen. The bottom line is that people are crazy.

I went home and made me a tuna hoagie and had my favorite low sodium lay's potato chips with it. Right as I sat down, Shaquan called me and asked me was I dressed?

"Yes son, I am. Why do you ask?"

"Me and Serg. is walking up the stairs and I'm about to walk in."

"Okay."

They walked in, "What's up Mom?" he said as he kissed me on the cheek.

"Hey!"

Sergeant Harar gave me a firm handshake and said "Hello Ms. Valentine. It's nice seeing you again," he smiled while being overly friendly to me.

"Likewise Serg."

Serg. is in his mid-forties he is brown skinned with hazel eyes and he looks like he is around 5'5. He is nice looking but is not my type. He is the one who recruited Shaquan into the military. Serg. explained to Shaquan and I the positive benefits the military had to offer if Shaquan signed up.

Curiously I asked, "What brings you here today?"

With a partial smile, Serg. replied, "Shaquan and I are just hanging out before he goes to basic training next Friday."

"That's what's up," I responded.

Shaquan chimed in, "Mom I mentioned to Serg. sometime ago I was thinking about becoming a cop after I get out of the military."

Serg. now intervening stated, "When I was young my Mom was a single mother and one of her male friends took me under his wing and mentored me. Now he is a Commissioner at the 5th district. I decided to introduce Shaquan to him today."

"Isn't Pennsylvania fifth district the largest police department in the area?" I inquired.

"Yes Ma'am. Although he is not blood related I look up to him like a father and he has a lot of pull over there. I'm thinking after Shaquan finishes basic and decides to go forth in his career as a police officer he can talk to him. I'm just trying to look out for your son Ms. Valentine the way someone looked out for me.

Shaquan is on a good path and I'm going to do all I can do to keep him on the right path."

"Thanks Serg. I really appreciate you looking after my son."

"It's no problem, it's my pleasure to do so."
I smiled at Serg. and nodded my head.

Shaquan interrupted, "Mom we are about to leave before you really start talking and then we will never make it."

"Boy please."

"Mom you know you like to talk."

I snickered, "It was nice seeing you again Serg. I will see you later."

"Bye Mom, love you."

"Love you too Son."

I was thankful to God for sending a positive man to mentor my son who also cares about him. So many men and women lack good strong genuine mentors. Y'all we have to keep our children covered in prayer.

Our children are not perfect and neither are we as parents, but with love, structure and positive reinforcement our children will be just fine.

After they left I went to the mailbox. Aunt Hortez two cards where in there one for me and the other for Shaquan.

I also had a letter from Frank Hamilton a.k.a Flyez. How did Flyez get my address and what does Flyez want? I decided to open his letter later. I just didn't feel like dealing with my emotions concerning him right at this moment.

Chapter 19

Surprises

Today is sunny and bright. I'm in good spirits because today is Friday and Shaquan graduates from Cinnaminson High School. I'm super excited my first-born is going to graduate from high school.

Being a single mother and having a son, my worst nightmare was he would get caught up in the wrong crowd. Drugs, alcohol, gangs, being incarcerated or wrongfully killed by the police or his peers, these thoughts would try to torment my mind on a daily basis.

The only way I found peace was to stay in constant prayer. Today is a monumental moment for me while tears of joy flowed down my face. My cell phone ringing interrupted my thoughts. Ugh!!! Guess who is calling my cell phone. He just won't go away. Should I pick up the phone or not?

As I contemplated my cell phone continued to ring. "What," I answered with much aggression.

"Twinkle!"

"What Sly, what do you want?"

Sly replied, "Not you."

"So why are you calling my phone?"

"I'm calling for my daughter."

"Anisa is not here yet."

"What time will she be home?"

"Aren't you her father, you should already know the answer to this question."

Sly banged on me. Ten minutes later Anisa walks in.

"Hey Honeybun!"

"Hey Mommy!"

We greeted each other with a hug and kiss.

"Mommy! I'm so happy my brother is graduating today."

"So am I. Oh, before I forget your Dad just called for you."

"Dad called me while I was in school. I noticed I had a missed call from him when I got my phone out of my locker. I will call him back after I go to the bathroom."

I smirked, "Anisa you didn't have to tell me that."

Anisa chuckled.

I shouted, "Don't forget to wash your hands after you're done."

Anisa shouted back, "Mom I'm ten."

"Whoo!!! You are so old," I said while being playful.

I heard Anisa sigh while she shut the bathroom door. I guess she didn't think that was funny. But I did. Kids you know have a mind of their own.

I walked to my room into my walk - in closet. I picked out what I was going to wear for Shaquan's graduation. While Anisa is on the phone talking to her dad, she sits on my bed. I hear her saying something to her dad about Shaquan's graduation party tomorrow.

I really didn't care what she was telling him so I walked out of my room into the living room. I started to iron my clothes.

"Mommy, Dad wants to come to my brother's graduation party, but he is too scared to come because you don't like him."

"Anisa, this is the reason why I don't like him because he tells you stupid things like this."

"Dad also said he is having a graduation party for my brother tomorrow night."

"Oh really! Did your dad say where?"

"Yep, the party is going to be at his house. Are you mad Mommy?"

"Mad at what Honeybun?"

"Dad having a party for my brother."

"No, not at all. I'm sure your dad and Shaquan planned it together. We'll see how this party goes."

"Mommy are you going?"

"No, I am not. After we have Shaquan's graduation get together at Mikado's I will be coming home to chill with my Honeybun. We are going to watch Nellyville and all of the other shows we like."

Anisa said, "Yes!"

"Make sure you pick out your clothes for the graduation ceremony and freshen up before we leave."

"I will Mommy!"

"Give Mommy a kiss."

"I love you Mommy."

"I love you too."

My parents, Diamond, Anisa and I are at the graduation ceremony. While we were waiting for the ceremony to begin, Candi called me to congratulate me.

"Twinkle; although we don't talk often you will always be my little sister. While I was sitting on my porch Sly told me Shaquan was graduating today. I wanted to cuss Sly out because you know I can't stand him but being that I'm sober I just ignore a lot of things now."

"That's good Candi. I'm glad you're balancing your emotions."

"Twinkle you are so comical. I almost forgot to tell you. Flyez stopped by some time ago and he was looking for you. Gurl he is fine and real clean.

He is not in the game anymore. He pulled up in a mean silver Benz pumpin' gospel music. I was like okay Flyez. He told me he is living in Brooklyn, N.Y. and he came to Philly to visit some of his family. Twinkle don't get mad but I gave him your address and your phone number."

"Why Candi?"

"Because I think he is good for you."

"I just got a letter from him on Wednesday."

"What did it say?"

"I didn't open it. I was trying to figure out how he got my address and why was he mailing me a letter."

With confidence, Candi replied, "I gave it to him and you need to open it."

"I will Candi."

"Besides anyone that you deal with will always be better than Sly's sambo ass."

"Candi the ceremony is about to begin. Tomorrow I'm having a graduation celebration at Mikado's in Cherry Hill at 2p.m. come through if you can."

"Twinkle, I'm not going to be able to make it because I have a hair appointment."

"Okay, we will connect soon."

"Alright Twinkle."

After we hung up, I kept thinking to myself what does Flyez letter say. I started thinking is he trying to contact me because he wants closure. Anisa interrupted my thoughts.

"Mommy," she said, while tapping me on my arm "Look at my brother walking on the field."

We started clapping and screaming woohoo!!! As the ceremony is going forth, Diamond leaned over to me and said, "Sis I overheard your conversation with Candi. Real talk Flyez was always that dude."

"Yea, he was but I don't believe in going back."

"Really sis! It took you almost a decade to leave Sly and you talking about you don't believe in going back. Twinkle you know… I said with her you are something else."

When they called Shaquan's name I took pictures and yelled go Shaquan with much joy and excitement. I was a proud mom. While the ceremony is going on, Diamond and I are having small talk.

All of a sudden we notice a Caucasian male running naked across the field in full speed. I'm trying to cover Anisa's eyes with my hands. My mouth is wide open in amazement. Some of the crowd is laughing and others are in shock. This guy tried to hop the fence with his naked self and the cops apprehended him. Whew it's never a dull moment. That was a good laugh.

Now the ceremony is over. I'm taking pictures with Shaquan, my parents, Anisa and Aunt Diamond. Everyone was all smiles and the wonderful thing is nobody argued. Today was a good day in my Ice Cube voice.

When I got home I opened the card Aunt Hortez mailed me. The card was so beautiful and a tearjerker.

It read something like you are a wise, graceful and a great mother, may God continue to bless you and your children. Love Auntie. P.S. Keep up the good work.

Enclosed was two hundred dollars. I called my Auntie so quick but she didn't answer. I left a voicemail message. I told her thank you and I will be giving Shaquan his card tomorrow at his graduation celebration.

Anisa fell asleep in the living room, so I carried her into her bedroom and tucked her in. I walked back into the living room sat on the couch while holding Flyez letter in my hand. I'm looking at the closed letter like do I really want to read this.

Thoughts started to race through my mind. Do I really want to open this can of worms? Where I am in my life, going back is not part of my plan. If we were meant to be, we would already be. You can't move forward constantly looking in the rear view mirror.

I started to reflect on the crazy men in my life. Sly is crazy, Asurion is insane and Flyez wasn't too far from neither one of them. Immediately after my thoughts, I got a text from Asurion saying the, "the clock is ticking." I looked at the text with the scoopy doo face and said out loud this dude is definitely in the DSM IV book.

For those who don't know what that book is. Basically it is the diagnostic and statistical manual for people with mental disorders, used by clinicians and psychiatrist to diagnose psychiatric disorders. In laymen terms this dude needs professional help and medication. Being that I know this, I'm going to ignore this text message and open Flyez letter.

Here I go. Dear Lisa, by the time your Blossom eyes and soft hands read and touch this letter. I pray you will be in good spirits and you will be in good health. The reason for this letter is to make peace with my past which you were part of. I never meant to hurt you or leave you by yourself to fend for yourself. The day I got locked up you told me not to go into the store and steal. Although you didn't know what I was going to do you felt I was going to do something wrong. That day I got locked up I was transferred back to NY where I originally violated my parole. When I moved to Jersey I was trying to start off right. But the same thing I did in N.Y. is the same thing I did in N.J. I realized you cannot run away from your problems, but you have to face them to conquer them. I know it's been almost eighteen years since we have spoken. But I want to tell you I am sorry. I always loved you and I'm a changed man Twinkle. I'm one of the ministers at my church. I gave up the game totally and been out for fifteen

years. Here's my number, I'm living in Brooklyn and hope
to hear from you soon my sunshine. Peace.

I shouted, "Lord what am I going to do? Please
guide my decisions and footsteps."

I rationalized that calling Flyez wouldn't hurt
anything. I decided to call him tomorrow.

After I read the letter, I remembered I did do Flyez
dirty. I was supposed to wait for him when he got locked
up, but I started to mess with Sly. Not only did I mess with
Sly, I fell in love with him and had a baby by him.

What is Flyez going to say about that? I met Flyez
when I used to work at the nursing home. We both were
certified nursing assistants. When I met him Shaquan was
two months. I was nineteen years old and Flyez was
twenty- six.

He is originally from Central Islip, N.Y. but when
he moved out of his parents' home he moved to Brooklyn.
Flyez got in some trouble then moved to New Jersey. We
were only together for seven months but at that time it felt
like it was the best seven months I had with any man.

Flyez spoiled me with jewels and made sure
Shaquan was okay. Anything I wanted Flyez gave me,
actually he was saving for an apartment before he got
locked up. Flyez saved five thousand dollars and I spent it
all. I feel so bad now. Dang, I was young and dumb. Flyez
never called me out of my name when he realized I spent
the money. Nor did he diss me when I told him that it

would never work out between us. Flyez just left me alone. He always had a legit job but at the time he was hustling on the side. He is six-foot- one, medium build, with a bacon brown skin tone and light brown eyes. And I just love his New York accent. Flyez was very intelligent but at the time he loved the streets.

After reading the letter I started to miss him. Maybe I should apologize for spending all of his stash I wondered. Now since we've grown up maybe we can do it right this time. He loves Jesus and Candi confirmed it. I love Jesus so why not at least see where it will go. Flyez might be the one.

Shaquan is leaving next Friday and it will be nice to have a man check up on me and Anisa. Besides I still don't know what's going on with Asurion's mind. All of these thoughts raced through my mind. Sometimes I think I think too much.

Chapter 20
The Party

I finally drifted off to sleep. Early morning I was awakened by my upstairs neighbors howling, barking and whiny Jack Russel. All this dog does is cry and howl. I believe he suffers from separation anxiety. Every time Zak or Holly leaves, this dog will howl and it's non - stop.

One day I texted Holly because I got so fed up with her dog excessive howling and suggested maybe she should put her dog on doggy Prozac. Clearly, she didn't take my advice because the dog is still barking.

Eventually I got up and started moving around and called Shaquan to tell him Aunt Hortez mailed him a card and reminded him the graduation celebration will begin at 2p.m.

"Mom, I'm always on time."

"What are you trying to say son?"

"I hope I see you there at 2.pm."

"Shaquan you got jokes at 9a.m. I continued, I will be there before 2p.m. see you then."

"See ya Mom."

"Bye son."

I started to straighten up the house and asked Anisa did she want breakfast.

"I sure do Mommy. Can you fix bacon, eggs and toast?"

"I sure will."

As I was fixing breakfast I kept thinking about Flyez and if and when I should call him. I began to get butterflies in my stomach. I thought, Twinkle you are doing too much.

Sly hates me, Asurion is somewhere over the rainbow, now Flyez. They say the third time is a charm. Can he really be the one? God I need your help and direction silently I spoke, and please keep my hormones under subjection in Jesus name amen. While Anisa and I were eating breakfast my cell rings. I looked at my phone like… who is calling me now? It was Pricy.

"Hey Pricy," I answered.

"Twinkle," she replied in a stern tone, "What time does the graduation start?"

Happily I responded, "At 2p.m. are you coming."

"If Sly doesn't come," she said rudely.

I started to walk away from the kitchen table to my room because I didn't want Anisa to hear the conversation.

"Pricy really are we still on this?"

Pricy is not backing down. "Is he coming Twinkle?"

Now shouting, "No Pricy! Sly is not coming, do you feel better?" I repeated for the second time. "Sly is not coming and why are you so focused on him? Sly is not even thinking about you."

Pricy then hung up the phone. I walked back to the kitchen.

"Mommy are you okay?"

"Yes baby I am."

"Is cousin Pricy okay?"

"Yes."

Now redirecting the conversation, "This turkey bacon is bangin' Anisa."

"It is Mommy, turkey bacon is my favorite," she said; while holding the bacon up in the air. Then she took another bite.

Honeybun, Mommy is about to get my clothes ready. After your done eating get your clothes so I can iron them.

"Okay Mommy."

I looked at the clock and it was almost 1p.m. Boy time flies. Anisa and I started to head out to Mikado's. I left early because I wanted to set up some balloons and decorations in the room I reserved.

I wished Pricy was here to help me because decorating is her specialty. Being that she is trippin', I'm just going to leave her alone and hopefully she will find herself. Thank God Anisa enjoys helping me.

My family and friends started to show up around 2:30p.m. Everyone was socializing and enjoying good conversation. Shaquan showed up with his girlfriend Jha-maica. I think they are a very cute couple.

After Shaquan arrived, everyone started to eat. I set up a table where family and friends could place their cards and gifts for Shaquan.

"Mom," Shaquan walks over to me and whispers, "My other girl just showed up."

In disgust, I asked, "Why did you invite her?"

"Because, I didn't think she was going to show up."

"That's genius Shaquan."

"Mom what am I going to do?"

"I don't know, you should have thought about that before you invited her. What is her name?"

"I forgot, Mom."

"How do you forget your other girlfriend's name?"

"Because she is my 'other' girlfriend. The key word is 'other.'"

"My only suggestion is to tell Jha-maica the truth before "Other" does."

"Mom are you trying to be funny?"

"Well you are the one who forgot her name so I just gave her one. Let's call her "O" for short."

"Okay Mom," Shaquan said as he walked away.

Pricy walked into the room. I acted like I didn't see her. Diamond walked over to me, "Sis what's up with my neph."

"Your neph is about to get caught."

"Player's don't get caught."

"Oh yes they do, everybody gets caught. Diamond honesty is the best policy."

"Sis that ain't the player's law."

"What is the player's law?"

"Now let me break this down to you Twinkle. The player's law is not only the player's law but it's also the "presumption of innocence."

This is one of the most sacred principles in America, which is my favorite. You are innocent until proven guilty," she said with a mischievous grin.

Being frustrated I stated, "That's why there are a lot of people locked up now because what they did in the dark finally came to the light. It doesn't pay to be a liar and play mind games with people. It's all fun and games until someone gets hurt. People now days are emotionally disturbed and unstable.

My favorite rapper DMX quotes it best, "you do dirt, you get dirt." You know us Sagittarius be about that life."

"Okay Twinkle."

"Don't get mad at me because I'm telling you the truth. The truth sometimes hurt but the truth will also heal and help you."

Diamond redirecting the conversation, "Do you want a drink?"

"Yeah, give me a Sprite."

"I wasn't talking about a soda sis," she snapped.

"Oh! My bad, no Diamond I'm good."

Diamond walked away shaking her head. I got up and took some pictures with my parents, Aunts and Uncles. While I was walking to the ladies room I hear, "Twinkle, Twinkle."

I sighed and turned around with an attitude because I knew who was calling me. It was Pricy.

"Twinkle, I know you saw me when I walked into the room."

"I did. What did you want me to do?" It really wasn't a question. I was being nonsensical. "Find a podium and announce that Pricy is in the building so everyone can stand up and acknowledge your presence.

This chick started yelling, "I didn't have to come to Shaquan's graduation party. And you need to show me some respect and appreciation."

"Pricy are you having a bad day? And why is your wig on backwards?"

Now Pricy is trying to adjust her wig. I continued, "Every time your wig is on backwards that has always been my sign that you were using again.

This explains your erratic behavior. You usually start off with your wig being lopsided. Then gradually go all out to wearing it backwards. Pricy you missed a step; I guess you have the "F-it" attitude."

"F@#$ you and F@#$ this whack ass graduation party," Pricy yelled as she ran out of the restaurant slue footed.

This was one of the funniest things I've ever seen. Just picture this real quick, someone wearing a raggedy stiff wig backwards.

The bang is in the back and all of the rest of the hair is in the front and they are running slue footed. I got a good laugh out of that. I laughed all the way to the ladies room. Whew that was funny to me. As I'm walking back into the room I hear all of this commotion.

Jha-maica and "O" are arguing and throwing Lomein noodles and egg rolls at each other. Diamond runs and grabs Jha-maica I grab "O."

I directed "O" out of the room. "Hi, Sweetie, I'm Shaquan's mom what's going on?"

"O" started rambling; "I didn't like the way Jhamaica was looking at me. I felt like she was being disrespectful so I threw an eggroll at her like it was a baseball and it hit her big forehead. That's what she gets, next time she will recognize."

"Sweetie, I don't know what's going on but this is a no zone for violence. This is supposed to be a happy time not a hostile time; furthermore my son is not worth it."

"My bad, Ms. Valentine. But foreal, foreal don't that girl have a big ass forehead? Tell the truth, you can see her forehead from across the street."

Smiling a little I replied, "You're going to have to leave because I don't want anyone calling the cops. You know we are in Cherry Hill."

"I know Ms. Valentine I just can't stand her big forehead and when I saw my egg roll I couldn't resist. It was like something took over me. So I picked it up and threw it at her. You should have seen how her forehead moved into the egg roll. It looked like her forehead was about to open up and swallow the egg roll."

"Trust me I understand that emotion but we can't have that drama here."

I walked her out of the restaurant and told her to drive carefully. She got into her car and sped off. When I returned to the room the energy was off.

The older relatives started to say their goodbyes. This was good because it was almost 5:30p.m. Everybody was full and they got a show. I looked at Shaquan with such disappointment. Diamond was sitting down smirking.

Violence is not funny I thought to myself. It's ignorant and uncalled for. People need to grow up. Shaquan walked over to me and said, "Mom I had no control over the situation."

"Yes you did Shaquan, and you need to start taking responsibility for your actions." I yelled, "You never should have invited her point blank period."

"Okay Mom," he said as he walked away.

I started to wrap things up. Everybody started to say their goodbyes. Shaquan thanked everyone for coming out and supporting him. I thanked everyone as well. Shaquan loaded his car with the gifts and cards he received.

Chapter 21
Wake Up Call

Finally, Anisa and I are home, we unwind and watched TV. I drifted off to sleep around 9:30 that night and suddenly woke up around midnight. I woke up, because I felt like something was wrong with Shaquan. I just didn't feel right in my spirit.

I started praying God please protect my son from the seen and unseen dangers. I opened my Bible and read Psalms 91 which is the scripture I read when I feel like my children or I are in trouble.

I tried to go back to sleep. I tossed and turned. I decided to drink some warm milk. Besides that is what they do on TV. At first it was nasty but the trick is you have to add some sugar.

See, I just helped some of y'all out.

Shortly after I dosed off I was awakened by an unknown number.

"Hello," I answered in a whisper.

"Mom."

"Yes."

"I'm locked up."

"What! Where are you?"

"At the 5th district."

"Okay I'm on my way."

I put on jeans and a shirt. I brushed my teeth then woke Anisa up. I was driving so fast down Route 130 you would have thought I was the star in the movie *"Fast and Furious."* Thoughts raced through my head. Those girls set my son up. See this is what happens when you mess with people's emotions. I started to get so angry. I was thinking some girl probably lied and told the cops my son raped her. It was probably the girl at the party.

I finally arrived at the 5th district. I saw an officer and immediately explained to him who I was. The officer voiced that my son is in a holding cell.

"What happened," anxiously I asked.

"Ma'am calm down the Commissioner is going to speak to you shortly."

I started shouting, "Why can't you talk to me. You are standing right here."

"Ma'am" he said firmly, "Please calm down and have a seat."

I looked at this dude like you lucky my daughter is with me because I would go in your mouth. I sat down and now my foot is shaking and I can't sit still. Anisa is crying. I'm telling her to calm down because everything is going to be okay. Finally the Commissioner comes out. I stood up and gave him a firm handshake.

"Hello, Ms. Valentine, I'm Commissioner Ferebee."

"Hello sir, can you please tell me why my son is in here."

"Your son was driving under the influence and one of my officers pulled him over. The car your son was driving wasn't registered in his name and it was not insured."

"Whose name was the car registered in?"

"Shawn Murray."

Instantly I became outraged. However, I didn't say anything. The Commissioner continued, "When the officers checked the car they found a pound of weed in the trunk of the car." My heart dropped.

"Ma'am do you know who Shawn Murray is?"

"Yes I do, he is my daughters father. We have been broken up for some time but Shawn still stays connected to my son. Shawn has been in my son's life since he was a baby."

"Were you aware Shawn had a graduation party for your son tonight?"

"No I was not aware. What puzzles me is that my son has his own car."

The Commissioner stated, "Your son told us he had a headlight out on his car and this is the reason why he used Shawn's car to make a liquor run."

I thought to myself unbelievable.

"Ma'am we are not going to book your son. Your son has no priors and he was very respectful when he got pulled over. By your son's reaction, the officers believe he was not aware of the weed in the car. As a result, I'm going to let him go without charging him. However, we are going to go after Shawn."

"Commissioner, I can't thank you enough. My son is leaving next Friday to go to basic training; he signed up for the military."

"I am aware of this Ma'am. I had the pleasure of meeting your son a few days ago. Sergeant Harar and your son came to visit me. Your son is a good kid, Ms. Valentine keep up the good work."

Tears streamed down my face. "Thank you sir! Thank you so much."

"You're welcome," he replied as he smiled.

Shortly after, Shaquan was released from the holding cell. During the ride home all I said was I hope you learned your lesson. And I pray you are thankful and appreciate the favor which is upon your life.

He looked at me like he was scared and embarrassed.

I dropped Shaquan off at my parents' house and went home. I was angry and thankful at the same time.

I wanted to call Sly and cuss him out, but I decided to go to bed instead.

Chapter 22

Words of Encouragement

Today is Sunday and I couldn't wait to go to church. I was so thankful to God for looking out for my son. During the service I think I ran around the church at least seven times. I praised God so much I was sore after service was over.

God is good even on a bad day he is still good. The reality is sometimes strangers will treat you better than your own family. This is a hard pill to swallow but this is real. I found out a lot of family members want you to do well but when they feel like you are doing better than them this is when they begin to hate. The reality is jealousy is how a person perceives themselves in your presence.

For instance they will make comments like you think you're better than me. It's not that your better, you are just better then where you been. These people are just looking at your finish product. They don't know your story behind the Glory God has revealed upon your life.

They don't know about the thousands of dollars you invested and lost. They don't know that you were late on your bills and almost lost your house, because you choose to invest in your dream and walk by faith. They don't understand your sacrifices, sickness, late hours, sleepiness nights and roadblocks you've encountered to get to the place called fruition. They don't know how many times you felt like giving up. They don't understand how many times you asked your self is this all worth it? They don't understand the reason God is exalting you is because you remain humble before him.

Anyone who tries to make you feel bad for your accomplishments, anyone who hates on you, anyone who calls you self-righteous, anyone who speaks negative to you and about you, I suggest that you cut them off. Including family, because what they are dealing with is beyond you.

The bottom line is you cannot change anyone. However you can change who you choose to communicate with. Cut the ungodly soul ties loose and get delivered from people. Live your life the way God intended you to live it. And don't feel bad about it. Maybe if these people would get a life of their own they won't be so worried about yours.

The problem is, these people don't want to put in the hard work, these people are looking for something for nothing and they want a free ride on your expense. Not so.

The truth is; God is not selfish with his blessings. God delights in blessing everyone. Some decisions you make concerning your life everyone is not going to be happy about it. Well making them happy is not your responsibility anyway. Whoever wants you to live in misery for their happiness should not be in your life to begin with. Remember this, the good book states a peaceful heart leads to a healthy body; jealously is like cancer to the bones. Basically envy literally rots your bones. Proverbs 14 verse 30. Read it.

When you are in pursuit of your destiny, your walk is going to intimidate the weak. Again that is not your problem. You will never be good enough for everybody, but you will be the best for those who deserve you. Continue to be you. I encourage you, to be victorious and not a victim. I encourage you to pursue your dreams no matter what the naysayers and soothsayers say about you.

Let there lies be the fire that drives you to become successful. I heard the more successful you become the smaller your circle will become. This is true. I don't have a circle, I have a line of a faithful few who got me and I got them.

I don't play anyone close that is dysfunctional or unstable. When someone's negative vibes begin to infect your spirit it is time you chuck up your deuces. Some people are comfortable being damaged with a toxic lifestyle.

However you don't have to subject yourself to that toxicity. If you do, I promise you it's going to kill you slowly. Satan is the author of confusion and the father of all lies. If there is confusion in your atmosphere it is because a liar is lurking in your atmosphere. Pin point the liar and the confusion will cease.

Ungodly soul ties are very real y'all and so are demons. They will get into anyone who will welcome them in. I don't have time and neither do you. I'm on a rescue mission for souls who really wants it. If you don't, that is fine with me. Because I'm going to shake the dust off my feet and keep it moving.

Don't ignore the signs that God is giving you concerning some people. God has a great way of protecting you from people who don't mean well. Rejection is not only redirecting you to another direction but it is also God's way of protecting you.

Be mindful and be strong. Okay that was my words of encouragement to you all. Be blessed and I love y'all. Now let's get back to the story.

Chapter 23
What Do I Do?

Today is Anisa's last day of school and she is super excited. So am I, maybe I should enroll her into summer camp part time. Being that I'm still home. I'm not sure what I'm going to do with my Honeybun. However, what I am sure of is making that phone call to Flyez. I'm so nervous, what am I going to say? What is he going to say? I need to stop procrastinating and just call him.

The reason I'm struggling is because I don't believe in going backwards which is a pet peeve of mine. Every time I go back it never works out well for me. Something is telling me not to call him, but on the flip side something is telling me to call him. What should I do? I know someone just said Twinkle call him already.

Okay! I dialed his number then I quickly hung up. I know that was such a punk move. I rationalized, he is probably at work and I don't want to get him into any trouble. All of these thoughts came to mind. I'm just going to call him and if he doesn't answer I will leave him a message or maybe I should text him? No a text is so impersonal. I decided to call him again.

He answered, "This is Frank."

"Hey Frank."

"Is this Blossom eyes?"

"Yes it's me," my smile got brighter.

Blossom eyes is the nickname he gave me.

"How are you?" he said with excitement.

"I'm well, are you busy?"

"Actually, I'm not, I'm off today."

"Hmmm, what do you do?"

"I work for a glass factory in Brooklyn. My days off are Sunday and Monday. Twinkle, I didn't think you were going to call me."

"I was nervous Flyez, I didn't know what I was going to say."

"When did you become shy? The Twinkle I know always had or has something to say whether good or bad."

"Oh! Be quiet Flyez. A lot of things changed."

"I know Candi told me you have a mini you and Shaquan is seventeen. Wow! The last time I saw him he was in the car seat."

"Yeah, and now he is a graduate from high school."

"Blossom eyes, I never stopped thinking about you and I never stopped loving you."

Brushing him off, "I heard you were in church now?"

Flyez sounding proud, "You heard right, I am now a deacon and been clean for ten years. I changed my life around for the better. I went from negative to positive."

"Okay Biggie Smalls."

"Now that's the Blossom eyes I know." We both chuckled.

"Shaquan is leaving this Friday for basic training."

"Where is he going?"

"He will be stationed at Fort hood, Texas for six weeks."

"I know you are proud of him."

"Yes, very proud of him. Do you have any children?"

"I have no children."

"What! I said in disbelief. Did you ever get married?"

"No."

"Are you in a relationship?"

"No, Twinkle. I live by myself and you are welcome to come to New York anytime you like."

I was lost for words. Flyez peeped it so he broke the silence.

"I'm on my way to the church because I clean the church on Monday's."

"That's what's up."

"I try to stay busy doing things that are productive. Blossom eyes let me ask you this."

"What is it?"

"Are you still with your daughter's father?"

"No, and haven't been in a long time."

"Are you seeing someone?"

"No Flyez, I'm chilling and waiting on God."

"That's good," he responded he continued, "Can I call you this evening."

"Sure, I'll talk to you soon."

With urgency, Flyez said, "Blossom eyes" he hesitated.

"Yes" I responded.

"It was nice to hear your voice again."

"It was nice to hear from you to Flyez."

"See you later."

"Later."

After we hung up, I was amped. All of my old emotions started to awaken. I couldn't stop smiling. The girl Twinkle still got it. I said while doing the old school dances like the "cabbage patch" and the "wop." I think real love finally found me. Hearing Flyez voice made my liver quiver. I know that statement sounded like something a grandma would say about her husband. But that is how I felt.

Suddenly my phone rings, its Shaquan.

"Hey son!"

"What's up Mom?"

"Nothing."

"Mom I apologize for putting you through what I put you through."

"It's okay, we all make mistakes. Did you get your car?"

"Yeah, I had Jha-maica drive me to Sly's house."

"Shaquan there is nothing wrong with having fun, but you must be responsible. Thank God you were shown great favor because with that much weed, it's at least a two year prison term easy.

They could have got you on possession with the intent to distribute. Did you know weed was in the trunk of Sly's car?"

"No."

"Shaquan I don't know what's going on with you but something is not sitting right with me concerning you. I know Sly has been in your life for a very long time but he is not a good example for you. There is a time when people are supposed to grow up. Sly is darn near fifty and he is still hustling. Don't you think something is wrong with that?"

Shaquan didn't respond.

"The Bible says," now Shaquan interrupting. "I know Mom," sounding bothered.

"You know what Shaquan," I replied with aggression.

"When I was a child, I thought as a child; but when I became a man I put away childish things."

"Well, I'm glad you know the scripture now it's time for you to apply it. You have too much to lose and real talk you ain't about that life no way."

"Mom, I love you," Shaquan changing the tone of the conversation.

"I love you too. So Friday is the big day."

"Yeah, Serg. Is going to pick me up from grandma's house and take me to the base. Then from there a hotel."

"Why a hotel?"

"Because there is a shuttle that's going to take us to the airport the next day."

"Son, I just want the best for you because you deserve it. I know you don't want to hear it, but your mother is always going to tell you what's right and what's wrong. You might not like it, but one day you will appreciate it. As a mother sometimes the hardest thing for me is to tell you the truth because I don't want you getting angry. But at the end of the day good will always win over evil. The truth hurts but the truth will help you. Being a parent is the toughest job on earth."

"Why Mom?"

"Because I'm responsible for the physical, emotional and mental development of another human being. One day son, you will become a father and you will understand."

"Mom have you talked to Sly?"

"No, I have nothing good to say to him. Why do you ask?"

"He told me he was going to call you."

"Well he didn't and I hope he doesn't. What time is Serg. picking you up on Friday?"

"One - thirty in the afternoon."

"Okay, Anisa and I will be there on Friday to take some pictures and wish you well before you leave. In the meanwhile be careful. Talk to later."

"Later mom."

Chapter 24

Let's

Talk About Sex

As soon as I hung up Jelly called me.

"What's up Jelly," I answered.

Jelly went directly into the conversation. "Twinkle after our conversation we had when you took me food shopping. I decided to enroll in a dental assistant program."

"That's good news. I'm happy for you."

"I also decided to stop my profession as an oral sex teacher." Jelly continued, "I decided to sell sex toys instead."

"Jelly you are hilarious you just can't help yourself. You just have to have a hustle."

"Twinkle, I thought that was a better decision."

"Jelly, if you think that, than it is. I'm very proud of you."

"Twinkle will you come to one of my demonstrations?"

"No Jelly."

"Why not?"

"Jelly been there done that. I'm not trying to creep you out but have you ever heard of Astral sex?"

"Girl yeah, I love me some anal sex."

"Jelly, I didn't say anal," now laughing, I said "astral."

"Twinkle no, that's some new stuff. How do you know about it? Aren't you celibate?"

"Yes I'm celibate; however I do a lot of studying. Astral sex is the ability to project one's spirit man into another spiritual being while astral traveling. It's like this supernatural energy exchange which allows you to meet the spirit of someone between incarnations or a non-human spirit. This practice is straight crazy and is common amongst Satanist.

They leave their physical bodies in a dormant state while they project their spirit into the body of whoever is a participant in this satanic practice and they have sex. Then they have the nerve to have warning and danger signs. Which remind you to be mindful of the lower vibrational entities both human and non-human that will look to have sex with you simply to take advantage of you.

They believe that the lower vibrational exchange is not an even exchange but an energy of rape or psychic vampirism. The supernatural world is just as real as the physical."

"That's crazy Twinkle."

"It's real Jelly. There is also an entity called spiritual wives and husbands. These demonic spirits can enter in through masturbation and lust. Sometimes they will manifest in your dreams. These spirits are so deceptive they will use the face of people you are familiar with.

Have you ever had a sex dream and it was the bomb? Afterwards you wanted to call the dude well in your case maybe a chick?"

"Yeah, Twinkle I had one the other night and I called him and his wife had the heart to call me back. I cussed her out but the funny thing is she knows about me."

"Jelly just because she knows about you doesn't make it right."

"Twinkle that is why I learned to like you because you always keep it real."

"Knowledge is power. Did you ever ask yourself who was you really having sex with in the dream?"

"No, truthfully I was hoping I would have another dream. When I have dreams like that I consider them a treat."

"Jelly it's a trick from satan. The correct term is incubus meaning a male demon or succubus meaning female demon. These spirits seduce males and females through sexual activity often in your sleep."

"Wow! Twinkle!"

"Jelly if you don't believe me go on Safari on your phone and look it up. I'm not trying to knock your hustle. I'm just trying to drop some knowledge. Regardless what you do, I still got love for you. However, I won't compromise. I have not always been at this place in my life and I still struggle.

Nevertheless, my Grandmother was the assistant pastor of her church and never judged me. She loved the hell out of me and she believed that one day I was going to totally surrender to Christ. When I totally surrendered to Christ, I thought I was going to be the Christian girl who continued to have sex and then tell people that God knows my heart."

"Twinkle, What's wrong with you?"

"I'm just being honest."

"Twinkle the married dude is beeping in on my other line. Let me click over to see what this chump want. I hope he gives me some bread."

"Girl I know that's right. Okay, Jelly I'll talk to you later."

"Twinkle thanks for not judging me."

"Girl you good."

After we hung up, I prayed for Jelly's strength because I know how hard it is to overcome the spirit of lust.

Heavenly Father I pray every blood ungodly soul tie covenant entered into Jelly through demonic spirits will be cast out in the name of Jesus. I pray she will lose the desire of lust and I command the spirits to loose her and let her go by the power and authority of Jesus Christ my Lord in Jesus name Amen.

Someone prayed for me and the majority of y'all reading this, someone prayed and is still praying for you too.

Never forget the power of prayer even when situations appear not to be changing. Prayer does change things and people.

How do I know? Because it changed me and I'm still a work in progress.

Chapter 25

See You Later

Today the atmosphere feels good. The air smells sweet like summer. There is a beautiful breeze flowing and the winds are blowing a beautiful tune. The birds are singing a lovely song. And the ladybugs are gracing me with their presence. The red and blue jays appear to be playing catch a girl get a girl. And the flowers are extra colorful.

It's a bittersweet moment because Shaquan is leaving today for basic training. Although I'm excited, I have mixed emotions because I'm realizing my son is in transition to becoming a mature man.

Anisa and I are in preparation to go over my parents' house in a little while. I went to the store around 10:00 o'clock this morning to purchase Shaquan's going away card.

While I was out Flyez called me and asked me how I was doing? I told Flyez I was doing fine. I asked him why did it take him four days to call me back.

He stated, "he didn't want to start annoying me because he knows how short tempered I am."

"Flyez, I'm not short tempered, I just don't have time for games."

"Blossom eyes I'm not playing games. I miss you and I want to see you soon... real soon. How do you feel about your son leaving today?"

"I'm coping with it."

"I would have loved to see him before he left. I wish I would have known sooner."

"Flyez if you are still around, you will see him when he gets back from basic training."

"Dag! Lisa, that's how you're feeling about me?"

"No," I started to laugh, "It just came out the wrong way."

"Blossom eyes I'm a changed man and I'm not going to hurt you. I waited too long for this opportunity to come back around."

"Flyez," I said now becoming serious, "I'm sorry for spending your stash while you were locked up."

"Blossom eyes, there is no need for apologies. I apologize for not listening to you that day and leaving you in a messed up situation. I was only thinking about myself. I'm sorry you and your son had to go through that. I was never supposed to leave you."

" Flyez we live and we learn and we are still learning."

"Can we learn together Blossom eyes?"

My heart started fluttering and I began to get warm and fuzzy inside. I didn't know what to say.

"Blossom eyes are you still there?"

"I started stuttering… yea, yea I'm still here."

"Can I see you tomorrow?"

"Um. I'm not sure. I have to check on some things and will call you back later."

"Lisa, I hope I didn't scare you away."

"Frank please, I ain't never scared." But inside I was feeling so nervous. "I'll call you later this evening."

"Okay lady, I'll be looking forward to your call."

After we hung up, I was like whew! Jesus keep me near the cross. Jesus please keep my flesh under subjection, please.

Anisa and I are now at my parents' house. My mom ordered Shaquan's favorite Chinese food which is General Tso's chicken and shrimp fried rice. We ate and talked along with taking pictures.

Diamond finally arrived at 1:00p.m.

"Diamond, Shaquan's Sergeant is picking him up at 1:30p.m."

"Okay, so what's the problem? He's only going to basic training and then he will be back in six weeks. Chill regular sis."

"It must be nice to have a nonchalant attitude."

"It is Twinkle, maybe you should try it." Diamond now changing the subject, "Did you get your air fixed?"

"No and Anisa has been getting constant nose bleeds because of the heat."

This is the perfect time to ask Diamond if Anisa could spend the night tomorrow. Then Flyez can come over.

"Twinkle when are you going to get the air fixed?"

"Did you forget, I'm not working?"

"My bad sis… my bad."

"Diamond could you do me a favor."

"What you need some money?"

"No, I want to know if Anisa could spend the night over your crib tomorrow. And then I will pick her up Sunday morning before church."

"Twinkle you can spend the night too. I know you don't cope well in the heat neither."

"I'm good Diamond, I'm just going to relax at my house."

"That's unlike you, especially because your central air is broke."

"I have an air condition in the kitchen and it cools down the living room."

Diamond gave me the sister look. Like this is BS but if you believe that, then so do I.

"Twinkle you have never been a good liar because you are too candid. You are withholding information from me because you are up to something."

"Since you are psychic Diamond, what information am I withholding?"

"I think you are creeping."

"With who Diamond," I said while snickering.

"Hee haw and tee hee to you Twinkle. I'm glad you think it's funny."

"It is, because you don't even know what you are talking about. Remember, Diamond you are the one who said you are innocent until proven guilty."

"Twinkle when did you start playing mind games?"

"It doesn't feel good now does it Diamond. Are you starting to feel agitated and aggravated. Huh! Huh! Now you know how I feel when you withhold information from me. It feels like an itch you cannot scratch."

"Okay, Twinkle remember the words that came out of your mouth. 'You can't scratch every itch'. Who's tittering now? Don't scratch the itch Twinkle, don't scratch the itch. Bang, Bang, Bang."

Right then, Shaquan's Sergeant knocks on the screen door. "Come in Serg." I shouted.

"Hello Ms. Valentine," he said as he removed his hat before he entered into the house.

"Serg. I just want to thank you for everything."

"No problem, Ms. Valentine. Shaquan is a good kid."

"Please tell Commissioner Ferebee, I said thanks again."

Serg. just smiled at me.

We took some more pictures said are last good byes and prayed for Shaquan before he left. Before Shaquan got in the car we gave each other a hug and I kissed him on the cheek. I told him to be safe and be mindful. "Love you."

"Love you too Mom."

Diamond whispered something to Shaquan, what she said only the lord knows. Before we left my parents' house Diamond said she will pick up Anisa tomorrow around 6p.m. because she had to take care of somethings before Anisa stayed the night.

"Diamond, I can drop Anisa off at your house."

"That's okay sis, while I'm out, I'll just swing by to pick her up."

"Okay, thanks sis."

"Remember Twinkle you can't scratch every itch."

She then got into her car and drove off.

Chapter 26
Awkward

While we were driving back home, Anisa asked could she go over her friend Jordan's house. They are both ten and they praise dance together on the same dance team. Both of them were also in the same class during the school year.

"Anisa, how do you know Jordan is home?"

"Jordan texted me, she was bored and she doesn't start summer camp until Monday."

Me and Jordan's mother don't speak often, however we are cordial. I called Jordan's mom Tanisha, she answered her cell phone.

"Hello Twinkle."

"Hey! Are you aware our daughters are plotting an unexpected play date today?"

"Jordan mentioned to me she was bored."

"Is it okay if Anisa comes over for a few hours?"

"Sure Twinkle, That's works out for me so Jordan can get out of my hair."

"I know that's right Nish. Okay we will be there in about ten minutes."

"Okay, no problem. See you soon."

"Later."

Anisa is so excited she is about to go over her friend's house.

"Mommy what are you going to do while I'm over Jordan's house?"

"I'm going to chill. Why do you want to know?"

"I want to know because I'm not going to be there."

"Anisa you are so inquisitive."

"It's going to come in handy one day Mommy."

"It sure is."

Now we are pulling up at Jordan's house. The front door is already open and Jordan is standing behind the screen door with a big smile on her face. Before Anisa got out of the car, I told her to have fun and always be mindful.

"I know Mommy you tell me this speech every time I go to someone's house," she smiled.

We gave each other a kiss and I told her I loved her.

"Love you too," Anisa said while she was getting out of the car.

"Hi, Ms. Valentine," Jordan shouted as she opened the screen door.

"Hey Jordan. Have fun now."

Tanisha is holding the screen door open, I shouted while the passenger window is down, "Thanks for allowing Anisa to come over."

"Twinkle it's all good."

"What time do you want me to pick up Anisa?"

"No later than 8p.m."

"Okay! I'll be here around 6p.m. I don't want Anisa to wear out her welcome."

"Twinkle you are so silly."

"I just say the things people are thinking."

Tanisha laughed softly. I waved good-bye and drove off. When I arrived home, I called Flyez and told him he can come over around 7p.m. tomorrow.

"I can't wait to see you Blossom eyes. What do you want to do tomorrow evening?"

"Flyez surprise me."

"How are you feeling since your son left?"

"I'm feeling okay actually I'm going to take a walk after we hang up. I need some fresh air. I need to gather my thoughts."

"Twinkle he is going to be alright."

"Thanks Flyez, let me change my clothes and get ready to walk for at least an hour around my complex. I'll call you later."

"Take care Twinkle. Call me back after you finish walking," Flyez said while sounding anxious.

"Calm down Flyez, I will, after I finish walking."

"That's my girl you never miss a beat."

"Bye Flyez."

It was so peaceful while I was walking the air smelled fresh and the temperature was perfect. As I was walking I started to feel a bit overwhelmed do to Shaquan leaving.

So I began to walk faster, eventually I felt my endorphins kick in. I began to feel much better.

All of a sudden I heard "excuse me, excuse me." It never fails as soon as I get time to myself someone pops up.

I turned around with a fake smile and asked, "Are you talking to me?"

The well – favored dark-skinned girl with three parallel tribal scars on both cheeks responded, "Yes."

"Are you okay, I asked?"

"Yes, my name is Goitsemedime Mbeki, I just moved here from South Africa."

"Wow! Nice, to meet you my name is Twinkle. What made you move to New Jersey?"

"Recently, I received my RN licensed, I'm a pediatric nurse. I wanted to work in the U.S. for experience. I work at Children's Hospital in Philadelphia."

"That's an awesome Hospital; CHOP has a great reputation. You will definitely have a good pediatric career working there. How do you pronounce your name?"

"(Khoat say mo Dee meh) but you can call me Dime for short."

"Okay that's better for me Dime. What does your name mean?"

It means, "The Lord knows."

"Yes he does Dime, the Lord knows everything."

"Do you walk often Twinkle?"

"No, not really. Today I decided to take a walk because I had a lot of things on my mind."

"How about you?"

"I usually walk at 2:00a.m."

"Dime why would you walk so late?"

"I work from 4p.m. – 12:00a.m. When I arrive home I can't go to sleep so walking helps me unwind. Besides, I love to walk. Today I have off that's why I'm walking now."

"Dime walking that late is dangerous. Although this is a quiet neighborhood you just never know."

Dime looked at me straight faced showing no emotion, while her accent becoming thicker responded, "I have protection."

She said it like she was about to pull out a spear from the back of her spandex leggings.

I did not back down. I asked her, "What kind of protection do you have?"

"I have a Tiger."

"Sooo you walk with a Tiger at 2:00 in the morning with you?"

"The Tiger lives inside of me."

"That's what's up Dime we all have a wild beast living inside of us. I have a Gorilla inside of me."

Dime still staring at me replied, "My Tiger is my protection."

Okay, now this conversation is becoming socially awkward so I'm going to change the subject.

"What street do you live on?"

"I live on Pearlite."

"So do I, my number is 128. Welcome to the neighborhood, anytime you need anything feel free to stop by."

"Thank you Twinkle for being so kind."

"You're welcome. I'm glad we met, I usually stay to myself but it is always good to have a nurse on the team. Maybe I can get a Cheetah and walk with you sometimes," teasingly I said.

Dime did not think that joke was funny. She sucked her teeth and said, "See you around."

"Yes you will and again welcome."

I walked inside of my condo. I took a shower and took a good nap. By the time I woke up it was time for me to pick up Anisa. I never called Flyez back, when I did think about calling him back is was past 10:00p.m.

Just my opinion calling a dude after 10:00 just seems too late. I don't think the conversation will be clean at this time of the night. You know the freak in people really starts coming out around 9:30p.m. By 10:00p.m. It's all the way out.

Around 10:30p.m. I received a texted from Flyez, "I guess ur still walking."

I texted back, "Lol, in the bed night night."

"Goodnight Blossom eyes c u 2 morrow."

Chapter 27
Don't Take It Personal

My cell is ringing and ringing. Who is it? It is Saturday morning and I want to sleep in. I ignored the call. Ten minutes later my cell rings again this time I look to see who's calling me.

Lord behold its Flyez. I decided to pick up, "Yes Flyez."

Flyez overlooking my attitude. "How was your walk Blossom eyes?"

In my morning deep and raspy voice replied, "You called me at 9:15a.m. To ask me how my walk was. Flyez you could have asked me that question later on today."

"Sorry, Twinkle you were the first person I thought about when I woke up."

My voice still sounding deep and raspy, "My walk was refreshing. I met a new neighbor from South Africa? This girl told me she walks in the neighborhood at 2:00 in the morning because it helps her unwind."

Flyez wisecracking replied, "I guess she's not scared of lions, tigers and bears."

I am laughing a little, "I guess not, when I told her to be careful, she looked at me like she was about to pull out a javelin from her sports bra. Then followed up with 'I have protection'."

"What is her protection?"

Now I'm beginning to wake up. "Flyez I asked her the same thing, she told me she has a Tiger. I don't know; she is on some other stuff. She looks like she is in her late twenties and about that life."

Flyez asked, "About what life?"

"The life of jumping in a hole full of lions and fighting them for the fun of it."

"Blossom eyes," he said while laughing. "You have not changed one bit."

"I'm so serious Flyez."

"I know. This is why it is so funny." Flyez changing the subject, "Is our date still on for this evening?"

"Yes."

"Alright, I'm going to leave N.Y. around 4:30p.m. And probably arrive in Jersey around 6:15p.m."

"Okay, see you then. Call me Flyez when you are on your way."

"Alright, I will."

"See you soon."

After we hung up, I called Diamond to make sure she was still picking up Anisa at 6p.m. Diamond stated she was still picking Anisa up.

"I will be there a little earlier. She continued, So Twinkle, what are you going to do being that you will be home all alone?"

"I'm not sure sis. I think I'm going to chill."

"Is Sly coming over?" Bluntly Diamond asked.

"Really Diamond, Sly?"

"Yeah, did I stutter? Don't act like baby *muva's* don't go back to their baby *fava's*."

"Well, I'm not going back to him period. I don't fool with Sly. But if I did, the last time I checked, I'm grown. I pay my own bills up and through here. I can do whatever I want to do, real talk if I wanted too."

"Oh, Twinkle you sound like you got a little defensive. Did I hit a soft spot?"

"Nah, but at the end of the day, I don't question you about your lifestyle and what you do. So why would you insinuate and question me?"

"Twinkle you sounding real guilty about something. I just asked you a question."

"Well, like I previously told you," now elevating my voice. "I don't mess with Sly and I'm not going too."

"Alright Twinkle relax."

Then Diamond had the audacity to follow up and say "Maybe you should because you are too uptight."

"Alright Diamond, I will see you at six," and hung up on her.

Diamond called right back and said, "Sister don't take that tone with me because I was only kidding."

I replied, "Aren't jokes supposed to be funny? Well there was nothing humorous about your corny joke."

Diamond now trying to change the tone of the conversation, "Twinkle is your period coming on because your emotions are slightly higher than usual."

"Diamond, I have a lot on my mind."

"I love you Twinkle."

"I love you too Diamond. I'll see you later."

"Okay."

Diamond knows I'm up to something she just can't put her finger on it.

After the phone call ended, I started to clean up my room. As I was cleaning I noticed a loose long thick gray cable wire in my closet.

I don't know why this particular item caught my attention, but it did. I placed the wire next to my pepper spray. While I continued to clean, I thought, maybe I need a dog.

A male Rockweller would be nice. I need some protection up in here. Wishful thinking, maybe Flyez will be my protection.

Yeah, Flyez is going to be my protection. The thought of that made me smile.

My thoughts were interrupted by Anisa sweet high-pitched voice. "Good morning Mommy, what are you doing?" She said as she walked into my walk - in closet.

"Good morning Honeybun. I'm just doing a little cleaning."

As she sat on my bed with her feet dangling with a smile, "I'm glad I'm going to Aunt Diamond's this evening. Mommy are you sure you don't want to come over Aunt Diamond's too. We can have like a slumber party."

I giggled. "No baby, I'm sure. Mommy is going to relax this evening."

Around mid -afternoon I received a text from Flyez stating that he is on his way.

"Anisa did you pack your overnight bag?"

She huffed, "I been packed my bag." She responded as if she was aggravated with my question.

Later that evening my doorbell rings. Anisa runs to the door and asked, "Who is it?"

"Aunt Diamond."

"Baby go ahead and open the door for your Aunt."

"What's up niece," Diamond said as she walked in.

"Hey Aunt Diamond," a bright smile graced her face.

"Sis thanks for watching Anisa tonight, I really appreciate it."

"No problem Twinkle that is what Aunts are for."

"Diamond being that Shaquan left I have an extra house key. I'm going to give it to you in case of an emergency. It's always good for a trusted family member to have a key to your house."

Diamond responded, "True, true."

As I'm showing her which key is for the top and bottom lock?

Diamond began to become agitated, "Alright sis. I'm taking Anisa to a 7:00 o'clock movie so I'll holla."

"Excuse me Diamond, don't be rushing me."

I rolled my eyes. "Come here Anisa and give your Mommy a hug and a kiss. Love you and you have fun with your Aunt."

"Love you too."

A few minutes after they walked out of the door, I received a text from Flyez.

"I should be at your house in 15."

"Ok," I texted back.

I began to feel anxious; the anticipation was beginning to become nerve wrecking. A few minutes later, I heard someone walking up the stairs. I assumed it was Flyez. I looked through the peephole because I wanted to see what Flyez looked like. I didn't want any unexpected surprises.

You never know it's been a long time since I saw him.

To my surprise it was Asurion repeatedly stomping the bottom stairs, unbelievable. I ran to my room to get my cell phone because I panicked. By the time I walked back to the front door my door bell rung. I opened the door with a straight attitude and ready to tell Asurion off. When I opened the door, Flyez was standing there with a bouquet of edible arrangements.

I said to myself what is up with the edible arrangements? First Asurion now Flyez. Maybe I'm just buggin'.

"Hello Blossom eyes," he paused, "Are you alright?"

I was lost for words for a few seconds and just stared at him.

"Twinkle," he shouted, breaking me out of my trance. "Can I come in?"

"Sure, come in."

"Blossom eyes do I look that different?"

"No, No I just thought."

"You just thought what?"

"Never mind," changing the subject "The edible arrangements look so delicious."

"You smell delicious and you are more beautiful now than you were before."

"Thank you, you don't look to bad yourself ole' head."

We both smiled.

"Sit down and relax. Would you like something to drink," I asked while I put the edible arrangements in the refrigerator.

"Sure, a bottle of water."

"I see you still love your water."

"You remember that Twinkle?"

"I sure do. How was the ride?"

"It wasn't bad at all."

"Did you get lost?"

"No my GPS took me right here."

When, I sat down on the couch. Flyez asked, "When was the last time you went skating?"

"I can't remember."

"How do you feel about going skating tonight? I know you love music and dancing. Plus I want to see if your skills are still up."

"Flyez, don't sleep, my skills are still up."

We arrived to the skating rink; while we were there we skated, talked and laughed. It felt like Flyez and I never disconnected we both felt comfortable. Eventually, I started to get tired so we sat down. While we were sitting down, Flyez asked could he ask me a question.

"Sure what is it?"

"Why were you so nervous when you answered the door?"

"I was nervous because when I looked out the peephole I saw my ex- friend walking up the stairs. But when I opened the door you were standing there."

"Are you still dealing with him?"

"No, I never really messed with him. We went on one date and that was it. Dude was crazy and creepy."

Flyez and our eyes locked. My heartbeat sped as I took a quiet deep breath.

"Twinkle I used to dream about this day. I never stopped loving and thinking about you. This time I want to make it right and make it work."

While we were staring at one another his lips got closer to my lips. We started kissing and my hormones started jumping. As a result, quickly I pulled back.

He said, "Let's skate some more."

"I agreed."

After thirty minutes of skating, I told Flyez I was ready to go because I was getting hungry, it's almost 9p.m. Flyez suggested we go to this joint called Warm Daddy's in Philly. Although Flyez lives in N.Y. he lived in Jersey for a couple of years before he got locked up.

He knew how to navigate Jersey and Philly very well. Warm Daddy's is a small and intimate setting with great food. Accompanied with the live entertainment makes a very remarkable evening. We were jamming while eating. It felt like we started from where we left off. The connection and positive energy was definitely present, we both was at ease.

"Flyez why didn't you ever get married?"

"I was waiting on you."

Is he the one? Something keeps telling me, Twinkle don't go back. Maybe my standards are too high. I questioned myself. Should I make an exception just this one time? I don't know what I'm going to do. For now on I'm going to continue to enjoy my turkey wings, mac and cheese and cabbage with my old/new boo.

"Blossom eyes."

I answered, "Yes" and smiled.

"I'm ready to rescue you and be that missing part to your puzzle."

I wanted to say well what are you waiting for? Instead I politely responded, "Only time will tell."

"You are still a tough cookie."

"Yes I am; that's the reason why no one has gotten any of these cookies in a long time."

He smirked, "The food and entertainment here has not changed a bit, it's still live in here."

I nodded my head in agreement. All of a sudden, we both heard thunder.

"Flyez is it supposed to rain tonight?"

"I'm not sure, let me check my phone. According to the weather on my phone it states a severe thunderstorm warning."

"Maybe we should start heading out being that we are in Philly plus you still have to drive back to New York."

Flyez agreed. The food we didn't finish we took it home. When we arrived home, I suggested that Flyez stay for a while to wait until the storm pass. When we were in route back to the house the winds were dangerously high and the rainfall was extreme.

We got severely wet while getting out of the car running to into my condo. Flyez took off his wet clothes and I gave him one of Shaquan's shirts and sweats to put on. I took a shower, yes I did because I don't like the smell of rain and I wanted to freshen up. While I was showering, Flyez was in the living room watching TV. After I got dressed, I put on some sweats as well.

Although I had on Victoria secret sweats I didn't put on the sweat pants that have the word pink written across my behind. I didn't want to go there. Then I sat on the couch next to Flyez.

"Twinkle I might have to stay the night. You see how God works."

"Flyez you are funny. If you do stay the night you are going to stay right in this living room... by yourself."

"Pow!"

"That's not a problem Blossom eyes, I respect you and I respect myself."

"Good!"

"Now since we got that out of the way." Flyez repeated, "Now since we got that out of the way," while kissing my neck. He started whispering, "Twinkle I missed you so much."

"I missed you too." I started to get weak. Passionately kissing, I felt his hand moving up my thigh. I began to silently pray. "Jesus please make a way out of escape because if you don't it's going to go down and I mean all the way down. Amen."

Right then, I heard this loud thunderous noise and then my power went out. Really Jesus! That noise snapped both of us back into reality. Thank God we have flashlights on our cell phones. Flyez out loud said, "Jesus my bad."

I looked at him and shook my head.

"Twinkle, I'm sorry, my flesh was getting the best of me."

"Clearly, and now we are in here sitting in the dark repenting."

"Do you have any candles?"

"You know what I do. I have a couple of portable lanterns, battery operated candles and battery operated stick on tap lights."

"Why do you have so many gadgets?"

I chuckled, "A few years ago N.J. had a hurricane watch and I stocked up. Although we didn't get hit, thank God I prepared myself for such a time as now."

As I'm placing the lights and candles, Flyez walks behind me and starts kissing my neck from behind.

"Flyez" I snapped, "Didn't you get the memo a minute ago? My lights are out. What is it going to take for you to get it… a fire? I'm not kissing you, touching you or sitting in the same room as you. After I put these lights up, I'm going into my room and going to bed. It's late and I'm tired. Now either you can go home or you can keep your behind in the living room and go home after the storm settles down. Which one is it going to be Flyez?"

Pitifully he responded, "I'm going to chill and wait until the storm settles. Blossom eyes, can I get a hug before you go to bed?"

"No! Flyez, no! Then next, you will want me to read you a bedtime story. Goodnight," I shouted as I walked into my room and slammed the door.

When I laid down, I asked God for forgiveness and also thanked him for making a way out of escape for me. Then I went to sleep.

A couple of hours later I was abruptly wakened by a loud sound and heard Flyez yelling, "Yo! Yo!"

As I was getting out of the bed, I mumbled let me find out this dude is scared of the dark and is having nightmares. When I walked into the living room I noticed my window air conditioner was on the kitchen floor and Flyez is fighting an intruder.

I stood there for a few seconds in shock, and then I quickly ran into my room, called 911, and grabbed my pepper spray and the cable wire. Unexpectedly the lights came on as I ran back into the living room. It was then I realized the intruder was Asurion. I heard a gunshot and Flyez fell down.

Out of nowhere, I did a call of duty army roll, knocked the gun out of Asurion's hand by hitting his hand with the cable wire. Kicked the gun underneath the sofa and then pepper sprayed him. Asurion fell to his knees and I started beating him with the cable wire.

He started screaming, I started hitting him even harder. As I was beating him I said, "This is what you get messing with the girl Twinkle. You thought I was a punk. Look who's screaming now?

Yeah, punk look at you, you are on your knees yelling for your momma. She can't help you idiot."

My adrenalin was pumping.

Asurion was moving and squirming trying to get up. I started quoting the scripture; no weapon formed against me shall prosper.

Now I hear someone at my front door. I know it's not the cops thinking I'm supposed to open the door. When the door opened it was Diamond. She opened the door and Asurion mustered enough strength to run out.

Screaming in fear, "Yo! Twinkle what is going on?"

There was blood everywhere. I got a towel and applied pressure to Flyez chest. I kept screaming, "He shot him sis, he shot him!"

Flyez eyes started to roll back. Come on Flyez stay with me. While I was applying pressure I started to rebuke the death Angel and his assignment in the name of Jesus.

"You can't have this Man of God. It is not his time to go." I heard Flyez uttering. "I am healed by his stripes."

"Yes! Yes! Flyez you are. Stay with me, stay with me."

The police and paramedics arrived and started to work on Flyez. They got him on the cot and took him out into the ambulance. Diamond walked outside with me, everything was moving so fast. I tried to get into the ambulance but the police officer said I couldn't go because he had to ask me some questions. I was so discombobulated.

Anisa screamed and ran to me out of Aunt Diamond's car.

"Mommy are you okay?"

That is when I gained a sense of composure.

"Yes baby, do Mommy a favor. Calm down and go back and sit in your Aunt's car."

Anisa was hesitant; "I don't want to walk to the car by myself."

"Okay, Mommy will walk with you."

While we were walking to the car, Anisa started crying, "Mommy was that Daddy in the ambulance?"

"No, baby not at all."

"Why do you ask?"

"Daddy's girlfriend called my cell phone cussing me out and told me she knew that Daddy was over here with you. Aunt Diamond took my phone and cursed her out and told me Daddy's girlfriend was drunk."

"Baby, why was you up so late?"

"I had a bad dream about you, woke up and started to tell Aunt Diamond. While I was telling her, that's when Daddy's girlfriend called my cell phone. I think she thought she was calling your phone but called my phone instead. Aunt Diamond then tried to call you to tell you what happened but you didn't pick up your phone. So she decided to drive to the house because she thought Daddy was here."

"Baby, it's going to be okay. Give Mommy a hug and sit in your Aunt's car. I have to speak to the officers."

I noticed it stopped raining as I was walking to the officers. My adrenaline rush was beginning to die down.

Diamond walked towards me, "Sis are you okay?"

"Yeah, I'm doing a little better. Anisa told me what happened."

Diamond asked in disbelief, "That was the boy Flyez?"

"Yes."

"Sis I knew you were up to something but I thought it was Sly."

"I told you sis, I'm done with him."

Now the police are asking me what happened. I explained to my best ability what just happened. I expressed to the officers that I really wanted to go to the hospital to make sure my friend is okay.

The officer said just a few more questions we need to ask you. All of a sudden I hear a loud piercing scream while someone is running towards me. It was Dime. She

278

grabbed both of my shoulders. Her face was bloody and she was screaming hysterically.

In a panic I asked, "What's wrong Dime, what's wrong?"

The police tried to console her but she ignored him.

"Dime you have to tell me what happened to you."

Dime kept saying, "Her claws got him."

Frantically I responded, "What claws Dime?"

"Twinkle he attacked me but my claws got him."

"Dime I don't understand."

Instantly she calmed down but she looked like she was spaced out and her accent became heavier, "I have claws and ridges inside and when he pulled out it bit him like a piranha.

That's what happens to vicious animals." Eerily, she started laughing, she continued, "He cannot pee or walk and it's held firm by shafts of sharp barbs."

The police interjected, "Ma'am please tell me what happened, I want to help you. Were you attacked?"

With an evil glare, "If he tries to remove it, it will clasp even tighter."

Dime appearing to be delirious said, "Twinkle, I told you I have protection. I told you I have protection."

What the heck is Dime talking about?

Discussion Questions

1. Who is your favorite character? And why?
2. What chapter did you relate to the most?
3. Who do you think Twinkle is going to end up with?
4. Do you think Flyez is going to live or die?
5. What do you think Dime did to Asurion?
6. Is there someone you need to forgive?
7. Do you feel like you are Ungodly Soul Tied to someone?
8. Do you know that greatness lives inside of you?
9. Pursue your dreams; God did not gift you for you to give up.
10. Keep the Faith!

Stay Tuned for Ungodly Soul Ties III coming in 2016.

Made in the USA
Middletown, DE
15 October 2015